ARCANE MYTHOS

THE DARKLAND DRUIDS - BOOK THREE

NICOLE R. TAYLOR

1

———

I stood outside the library doors, my heart beating with a familiar rhythm of nerves.

Behind me stood *Salle*, the enormous willow tree that grew in the centre of the Warren—the crystal cave that the Darkland Druids called home—her branches whispering comforting words in the artificial breeze.

I hadn't been this worked up since I was forced to do a presentation in front of my year eight English class. Shaking hands, cold sweat, laughing classmates —the horror was still etched in my long-term memory, and now I was having flashbacks.

At least I'd come up a little in the world. How many school bullies grew up to find out they had magical powers? *Not many.*

Rory appeared beside me, his messy brown hair artfully arranged. He also had on his best shirt and smelled like he'd dabbed on a little aftershave. Actually…I sniffed.

He peered at the wooden double doors. "What are we looking at?"

I raised my eyebrows.

"What?"

"What's that smell?"

He puffed out his chest. "My natural musk."

"Can you promise me something?"

"Anything."

"Never refer to your smell as your 'natural musk' ever again."

He laughed and knocked his shoulder against mine. "*Gealladh*."

"I'm nervous," I admitted.

"It's been like five minutes since you saved everyone. Besides, Delilah is your grandmother." He waved his hand. "You'll be fine."

I sighed, resisting the urge to roll my eyes. Defeating the Chimera on Earth had been a joint effort, but until I'd arrived, the Druids hadn't stood a chance against the fanatical Fae sect. It was the unexpected addition of my Fae powers that had managed to end the hunt.

Though, technically, it wasn't over. The Chimera were still hanging around…they were just *imprisoned*.

Now I stood on the precipice of petitioning the Elders for yet another favour. This time, I wanted to ask permission to go to the Fae realm to learn about my unknown Fae family, hopefully find out the fate of my mother, and possibly fight the Chimera on their home turf. Not to mention ask for an alliance with the Fae themselves—the good kind, that was.

It was going to go down a treat.

"I'm having second thoughts," I muttered. "What if they say no?"

"The Chimera can't come back to Earth without passing through the Witches portal in Ireland," Rory said matter-of-factly. "They can't hurt us here anymore, thanks to you."

"Thanks to us all," I muttered.

He held up his hands. "Hey, just calling it as I see it. We wouldn't have been able to imprison a legion of doomsday Fae in a prison inside death if it weren't for you."

Oh yeah, courtesy of the prophesied black sun.

"If I go, it will be as a half-Druid," I told him. "That comes with certain responsibilities. There will be no more anonymity for the Darkland Druids if I set foot in their world."

"Hmm," Rory murmured, "you're right. What a conundrum."

I stared at the door, afraid to open it. I didn't want to cause any more trouble, but there was a hole inside me that would always be empty…unless I found answers to fill it with.

"You know, understanding the implications of your actions will go a long way with the Elders," Rory continued. "Tell them what you just told me."

"Easier said than done."

"C'mon. Better get it over and done with or we'll be here all day." The Druid opened the doors and ushered me inside.

The library was a large, round room with thick emerald carpet—which, coincidentally, matched the colour of my hair—tall bookshelves inset to the wood-panelled walls, and crystal sconces dotted here and there. Desks and various seated areas littered the open space, separated by glass display cases full of delicate artefacts from the tumultuous past of the Darkland Druids.

The crowning jewel was the crystal dome. Brilliant purple amethyst glittered overhead, giving the illusion that the library existed inside a naturally formed geode.

The Elders—Shor Elinian, Rowen Ariennir, and my grandmother Delilah Odhweine—sat in the centre of it all, softly talking amongst themselves. After the events of the last week, they had a lot to discuss. Rebuilding their lives in Edinburgh after my father disturbed their solitary peace, for one.

They looked up as we approached, unsurprised that we were here. It was always that way with the older Druids—they seemed to know what we'd do before we thought about doing it. As Rory had taught me, it was about the journey and the lessons learned along the way, not the final destination.

Ignis—the tabby cat construct that housed a shattered human soul—sat in Delilah's lap, snoring loudly.

"He sits with me while I crochet," the Elder said with a wide smile.

"*Ignis*," I groaned.

The cat's paws twitched, but he didn't stir. To look at him, one would think he was a sweet house cat, not a magical web of prisms that his soul could weave into a face mauling tiger.

"He used to be a warrior in his human life, did Elspeth tell you?" Rory asked. "He sacrificed his soul to save a whole world."

"No," she said, giving me a stern look, "she did not."

"He Spirit Walks with me into death," I told her. "He showed me there."

Delilah stroked her hand along Ignis's curved spine. "Interesting."

"Shouldn't you two be out celebrating?" Rowen asked.

"The young have put a great deal of effort into their party this evening," Shor said. "Go, enjoy yourselves."

I began to fidget. "Well, I have something I'd like to…Well—"

"Elspeth," Delilah said, "there is nothing you cannot say to us. Not after the battle we fought together."

Nodding, I tried to collect my words. I'd overthought it so much, it was all jumbled in my head. *Simplify, Elspeth.*

"I'm here to ask your permission to travel to the Fae realm." I swallowed hard. "But…"

Shor raised an eyebrow. "But?"

"If I go, the Druids won't be a secret anymore. My blood will mark me there, just as it did here." *And a whole new world of problems would arise.*

Rowen nodded, understanding my meaning. "You're afraid of drawing us into another battle."

"My father may have brought the Chimera here by accident, but this… I could change everything for you again."

Shor cleared his throat. "Elspeth, we had an identity here for hundreds of years before the Chimera came. Twenty-five years is a small amount of time in a Druid's life. We can regain the meaning we lost while forging it anew."

"None of us will ever be the same," Delilah added, "nor should we. Life is constant change."

"Learning, understanding, and growth," Rowen finished. "That is the Druid's way."

"You forgot harmony," Rory quipped.

"Well, we can't forget *that*," Shor said with a smile.

I had to do a double-take. Grumpy Shor was cracking a joke? Stranger things had happened, I supposed.

"And how do you propose you will get there?" Delilah asked, glancing at Rory.

"The right way," I blurted before Rory could put his foot in it. "Approach the Witches and ask."

"And if the Witches allow you to cross, what is your plan?"

"I thought I'd go see whoever it is that rules the Fae. Ask for help, permission, whatever."

"You want to know your Fae origins," Delilah said, bowing her head.

"I'll always be a Druid," I said quickly, sensing a sadness in her voice.

"Of course, you will," she told me. "But we do have to consider the implications this will bring us here on Earth."

"And, as far as we know, the prophecy holds weight with the Fae," Shor commented. "A prophecy that still encompasses our people, Elspeth."

"Are you sure it's wise?" Rowen asked. "Your journey won't be easy, regardless."

"I know," I told her. "But how far can I get in an unknown world before something bad happens? Stabbing in the dark almost cost us everything."

If it weren't for Yenris'del—the Fae who'd once helped my father escape their world—I wouldn't have even understood the truth of the power I controlled. No matter her betrayal, she had helped me see the danger of my actions. I could have torn the veil between life and death, then the Chimera would have been the least of our troubles.

"What about an alliance?" Rory asked. "We present ourselves to their leader and explain our troubles with the Chimera. They pose the same risk to that world as they did here. Elspeth can help them.

We can propose an exchange of information. Make the first steps at contact."

"*We?*" Delilah gave him a look.

"Nations have ambassadors," the Druid said with a shrug. "Why not us?"

The Elders' expressions were unreadable as they glanced at each other.

"This has taken an unprecedented turn," Shor stated after a moment. "This is a path that does not promote peace. The Fae will want to go to war with the Chimera."

"If they're not already," Rowen mused.

"They will try and use you the same way we tried to force you, granddaughter," Delilah murmured.

"I can't just go there and hope everything will work out," I argued.

Rowen nodded. "Yes, but this is about us all."

"If Raurich goes, he faces the same dangers your father did, Elspeth," Delilah said. "And you face being turned to darkness by a much more powerful force of Chimera. In their own world, their power is unlimited, and their number… likely legion."

"I know it'll be dangerous," I said. "I know… I… The Chimera could come back here. They will keep trying. Once they figure out that we defeated them, they might send a double agent through the portal in Ireland, then—"

"Elspeth," Shor said gently, "a multitude of things could happen. Dwelling on them will not help."

"So what do I do?" I asked, tears stirring in my

eyes. "Half of me is missing and while the Chimera still live, the prophecy——"

"Screw the prophecy," Rory declared, taking my hand. "You've proven time and again that you have the power to defy it."

"That's not the point."

Rory snorted. "This is about more than some fancy words written on some flaky old parchment." He turned to the Elders. "I believe that Elspeth can not only rewrite it but destroy her so-called 'destiny.' This is about more. It's about identity, something the Darkland Druids know a great deal about." He raised his eyebrows at the Elders. "Perhaps our future meaning lies not with the homeland, but with stepping out of the shadows and back to where we used to stand... at the side of kings and queens, guiding them into peace and harmony. *Dearbh-aithne.*"

Rowen glanced at the other Elders. "Elspeth is the bridge between worlds. Perhaps that has another meaning."

"Well, Raurich has said the most intelligent thing in this room today," Delilah declared.

"You say that like you didn't think I was capable," he drawled.

"It's something I think we should dwell upon further," Shor said, ignoring the Druid. "An alliance with the Fae would have to be proposed delicately."

Delilah nodded in agreement. "They would have much to gain from us, but what would we gain from them?"

"Portals," Rory said. "We can open them, but we've forgotten how to find an address. Maybe they can help."

"An exchange of ideas is more than just getting something out of each other," I stated.

"You're correct," Rowen said, bowing her head.

Ignis lifted his head and when he saw me, he meowed loudly.

"Perfect timing, flea bag," Rory quipped.

Delilah laughed and shooed the cat away. "Go. All of you. Enjoy the party and do not fash. All will be decided soon enough."

Ignis leapt onto the carpet and brushed up against my leg.

I smiled and nodded, though my stomach still churned. We'd made our argument and the Elders would pass their decree. If I truly wanted to go, they knew they couldn't stop me, but I'd rather not go against the powers that be. I'd caused enough heartache around here, that was for sure.

"C'mon," Rory said as he led me out of the library. "You haven't lived until you've been to a Druid party."

That evening, I sat underneath the branches of *Salle* as the Druids celebrated the victory over the Chimera.

Rory had talked up the party like it was some kind of rager, but in actuality, it was pretty tame.

Music echoed off the gemstone walls as everyone laughed and danced. It was a sight I'd never seen in the Warren before. Everyone moved with ease now that the weight of the constant fear of discovery was gone.

Tables had been set up at one end of the cavern, each laden with a variety of food and drink. Bright green vines and colourful flowers had been woven into garlands and wreaths, and crystals glowed blue and purple like magical fairy lights in a fantasy forest. *Salle* towered over it all, the branches of the great willow tree sparkling in the crystal light.

It really was magical, and as I watched over the party, I couldn't quite fathom how I'd gotten from my tiny house in Sydney, Australia to a crystal cavern underneath Edinburgh.

If only Dad could see me now.

I sipped at the cup of flowery punch in my hand, watching as Ignis—in his tiger shape—sat in the centre of an admiring circle of Druidesses, as they stroked his fur and gushed over his handsomeness. When they began to weave flowers into his hair and drape a garland of coloured daisies around his neck, I had to hold in my laughter.

"That cat has no shame," Rory said, sitting beside me. "He's got more game than me."

"He's a total ladies' man." I chuckled and shook my head.

"Is that Arnold's punch?" He peered into my cup. "Careful with that… it's deadly."

Arnold was the self-appointed chef of the Warren and took great pride in everything that came out of his kitchen.

"This is my first and only cup." I grimaced and rubbed my palm over my chest. "I can feel the alcohol burning through my nerve endings."

"How are your brain cells?"

I frowned. "Why? Have you heard something?"

"I hear a lot of things."

"*Rory*."

"Okay, okay. Delilah has some good news for you."

My heart skipped a beat. "They said yes?"

"It didn't take them long to see that our request was reasonable." He puffed out his chest and grinned. "You're looking at the newly appointed ambassador for Fae relations."

"We're going?" I was equal parts terrified and excited. "You and me?"

"And Ignis, if he wants to go."

I went to throw my arms around Rory's neck, but I spotted Vanora sitting across the cavern, glaring at us.

"What about Vanora?" I asked. "This won't be a short trip, Rory. We could be gone a long time. I don't want to do anything to upset the balance between you two."

Long before I'd arrived, they'd been matched as a

genetic pair—a kind of arranged marriage—and according to Darkland Druid decree, their duty was to ensure the continued survival of the species. It was awkward to say the least.

It wasn't like I had feelings for Rory. We had a close relationship because of the things we'd been through together. He'd been my guardian—my *neach-gleidhidh*—and fought beside me as I'd discovered the true depth of my powers.

But no matter what I did, it didn't stop Vanora's jealousy. Not even saving her from dying a slow, painful death by poisoning changed her opinion. She loved Rory, but Rory had turned towards me while her arms were already open. Him leaving to go to the Fae realm on account of my personal mission was just another nail in her love story's coffin.

"Vanora will understand in time," Rory replied. "This is who the Druids are, Elspeth. We travel, we advise, we learn. It's not like our lives are as short as a human's."

"Have you already told her?"

He nodded. "Aye."

"I gathered. She's glaring at me with renewed dislike."

Rory sighed and took the cup from my hand, then drained the punch.

"Careful," I warned. "I don't know what's worse, the headache you'll get from that stuff or Vanora's wrath."

"*Tha e ro anmoch a-nis*," he drawled. *It's too late now.*

"Go," I said, nodding in Vanora's general direction. "We'll have plenty of time to talk, but there's nowhere near enough for her."

Rory muttered something in Gaelic under his breath and pushed to his feet.

Sighing, I watched him approach Vanora and wondered if I was doing the right thing by going to the Fae realm. The more I thought about it, the more anxious I became, though I knew that deep down I would never feel at peace until I knew what it meant to be Fae—even if I was only half. Not only that, but I needed to find out what happened to my mother. I knew she was likely dead, but a part of me hoped that she might still be alive.

And if she was… would this be the last time I saw the Warren? Only time would tell.

A dark shadow appeared before me and I blinked. Jaimie Fraser leaned down and offered me his hand. The hulk of a Scotsman had a tough exterior, with his bushy black hair and scratchy beard, but was the kindest Druid I knew.

"Ach, lass, I don't like that look on your face," he said. "Come and dance with me."

"Dance?" I blushed and shook my head. "No way."

He grinned and grabbed my hand. "You'll never escape me, lass. Prepare to be dazzled."

It was the last thing I thought would ever come out of his mouth, and I burst into fits of laughter.

Damn, I was going to miss this place.

2

———

The lush fields of Ireland flashed past as the hire car hurtled down the motorway.

When we'd finally departed Edinburgh—after a tearful goodbye from the Darkland Druids—I was surprised to find Rory knew how to drive.

We had to travel all the way to Holyhead in Wales in order to get a ferry to Dublin. I'd never driven onto a boat like that before, so I'd sat wide-eyed as we'd queued with other cars, busses, and trucks. They all fit into the belly of the ship like pieces in a game of Tetris, the vehicles waved along by workers wearing high visibility clothing.

Upstairs was a deck with lots of seats, a café, shop, and bathrooms. I'd made Rory go outside as we crossed the sea, the icy wind buffeting us as I leaned over the bow to watch the powerful hull rip through the water.

Now we were on our way to the County of Sligo in the west of the country. Supposedly, that's where we'd find the portal and the Witches who guarded it. We were operating on a lot of hearsay lately, and while it'd all work out so far, there was no telling when our luck would end.

Ignis slept on my lap, using the inside of my bag as his bed. He'd shrunk in order to fit and hadn't been impressed when Rory joked that he was travel-sized. I stroked the cat's back, thankful he'd decided to come.

When Rory turned off the motorway, my stomach did a flip.

"What do you know about the Witches exactly?" I asked.

"They call themselves the Crescent Witches," he replied. "Their covens have different names to symbolise an affinity for their magic. Apparently, they've lived in the same village for at least a thousand years."

Derrydun. "There must be something special about that place, then."

"Aye, their portal. They say they grow trees over them to keep them protected."

I blinked. "Trees?"

"Great hawthorn trees," Rory told me. "They seem to respect nature, at least. Didn't help when they decided to let the Fae have their powers back."

"Careful," I warned. "I know you're angry with them, but they don't know we exist. They probably thought they were doing the right thing."

Rory snorted. "Aye, well, I suppose we'll see about that."

I knew better than to argue with him about it, so I let the conversation go. The Witches were only one stop on the way to a bigger struggle—the Fae.

"Do you think the Fae will know more about the black sun?" I wondered aloud.

"More than likely," Rory replied. "It is a Fae ability and if you inherited it from your mother, then it's likely there have been more like you."

I swallowed hard. "I doubt they come with their own prophecies."

"I don't mean there's a whole family of veil wielding, green-haired goddesses," he went on. "I've always thought it was more of a selective ability."

"Or it was bred that way by whoever rules there. The Elders were right… they'll try to use me."

"You got out of it with us."

"I know, but—"

"The Fae are an unknown," he said with a nod. "You're smart, Elspeth. I know you will never let anyone use you. Besides, dwelling on what might happen is only upsetting you. Most of it will never come true."

I looked out the window. "I know. I'm just a gifted over thinker."

A sign ahead read: Derrydun (*Doire Dún*) 3. Not long after, the first signs of human habitation made themselves known.

The steeple of an ancient grey stone church

peeked above the thick forest, and I managed to make out all the headstones as we drove by. Crumbled and worn Celtic crosses loomed over smaller monuments dotted all over the brilliant emerald grass.

A cottage nestled back off the road flashed by on the right, and finally, the village centre appeared around a bend. Then—

"*Och, daingead!*" Rory cursed as he veered sharply to the left, then sharply to the right.

We came to a screeching halt in a parking lot beside a hot pink cottage with a thatched roof.

"Was that a tree?" I asked, looking over my shoulder.

"Aye," Rory said. He clutched the steering wheel so hard his knuckles had turned white. "They could have given us some warning. That's dangerous!"

I gave him a moment to breathe. "Well, I guess we can park here." I opened the door and climbed out, my boots crunching on the gravel underfoot.

I breathed deeply, my senses filling with the wild nature of the little village. Behind the pink cottage— which turned out to be a café and teahouse—was a babbling brook with a fairytale vibe. The main road was dotted with craft and local produce shops and an old traditional-looking pub. It must be a tourist town, which was curious considering who was supposed to live here. Somewhere in the woods behind all of this was a portal to another world.

Up the road, I could see a service station and a

single set of traffic lights. They changed to amber, then red, but there were no cars in sight. In fact, there was nobody on the street at all.

I frowned at the tree growing in the middle of the asphalt. There was a strange power lingering in it, one I hadn't felt even in *Salle*.

"That's a hawthorn," Rory told me. "They're sacred to the Witches, apparently."

I snorted. "So scared that they let one grow in the middle of the road."

"This whole place is strange," he mused. "Do you feel that?"

I stilled and closed my eyes. Not so long ago, I would have assumed it was the Chimera, but I knew they were safely locked away in the prison world I made for them in death. That meant this could only be Fae magic I was feeling.

"There's magic in everything," I murmured. "It's… sticky, like honey."

Rory nodded. "They certainly aren't afraid to use their powers here."

"I don't understand. Aren't there humans here? Or is the whole place supernatural?" I looked up at the ruins on the hill behind the village. A beacon burned at its apex, but it wasn't one that could be seen with one's eyes.

Fluttering pulled my attention back to the street. A white falcon with dusty tipped wings landed on the roof of the shop across from the teahouse and peered down at us. It tilted its head to the side, its black eyes fixed on Rory and me.

I didn't have to call on my power to understand that there was more to the bird than met the eye. I'd seen Jaimie shapeshift a few times, and I could see the subtle tells that marked him as a Druid. The way he held himself, the way he walked, the intelligence behind his big, brown, doggy eyes. It was the same with the falcon.

They were watching us.

Rory pressed his shoulder against mine. He sensed it, too.

I pressed my hand against the hilt of my knife for comfort. It was secure in its scabbard at my hip, the illusion that hid it intact.

Rory pointed across the street. "Do you think that's where we should begin?"

The store was called *Irish Moon*. A sign with a crescent moon hung from an iron bracket fixed to the stone and it creaked as it swung ever so slightly in the breeze. *Crescent Witches.*

I nodded. "Let's make ourselves known."

I didn't bother looking for oncoming traffic as I made my way to the shop. Ignis wriggled inside my bag but stayed put, content to let us do all the work before revealing himself.

Peering in the window, my curiosity spiked as I saw the treasures within. A cluttered display of crystals sat on a layered bed of black velvet—geodes, points, polished orbs, carved figurines, and tall amethyst caves that reminded me of the Warren. Behind them, I could make out the shadow of shelves stuffed with books, a rack of wind chimes, a counter with more crystals, and Irish-themed knickknacks.

There was also movement. A woman was waiting within, manning the till in case any customers decided to stop by.

A bell rang out as I opened the door and the woman looked up as we entered.

The first thing I sensed was the radiating energy from the crystals. It was so powerful that I felt the beginnings of a headache coming on. The second thing was the magic burning inside the woman.

Tarot cards lay on the glass before her in an elaborate spread, her fingers tracing over the image in the centre as she peered at us with brilliant blue eyes. She had to be around our age, early to mid-twenties. Her long, straight, indigo hair hung to her waist, though she held her head chin slightly downward, so it hung like a curtain around her face. It wasn't enough to hide the twisted scar that marked her from eyebrow to jaw on her left side. I wondered what had happened to her.

I shifted uncomfortably and nudged Rory. "The crystal."

"Aye, I feel it, too," he murmured. "It's a Druid thing."

The woman looked me over with a raised eyebrow, then turned her attention to Rory.

"If there's a secret password, we don't know it,"

Rory said to her. "So, let's just cut to the chase." He spread his arms out. "Take us to your leader!"

The woman snorted, her lip curling in amusement. "And what are you exactly?" Her accent was musical and so very Irish. Her gaze fell on me, then to my bag where Ignis hid. "I can sense the Fae in you, but there's something else… Something he has." She looked at Rory again.

I supposed she wanted us to tell her but introducing ourselves seemed to be the polite thing to do before any of that.

"I am Elspeth Qu— I mean, I'm Elspeth Odhweine and this is Rory—"

"Maerinn," he finished for me. "And you are?"

"Sage Williams," she replied.

When no one was forthcoming about their supernatural identities, Sage shook her head. "Do you know what this card is?" She held it up so we could see.

It pictured a jester juggling and Rory pouted. "The Fool. It's written right there. Are you trying to imply something?"

"The Fool isn't about stupidity," Sage told him. "It is the first and last trump card in the tarot. It symbolises a new beginning and an end to something in your old life. A new cycle begins." She smiled at me. "I haven't seen this card in a long time. Interesting that I drew it today, don't you think?"

"We don't divine," Rory told her before he turned to me. "See? I told you they were wishy-washy."

I slapped him on the arm. "She can hear you."

"Elspeth here has sense," the Witch said. She gathered the tarot cards and put them back into a little black box. "I suppose you'll be wanting to speak with my mother, then."

"Your mother?" I asked.

"To be sure. She's the matriarch of the Crescents. What she says goes. If you want to petition, she will hear you."

"Petition?"

"Aye," Sage replied. "Fae don't really come here unless they're invited or they want something."

"Why not?" I wondered. "I thought you…"

"I think you should ask my ma about those things," she said with a wave of her hand. Rising, she rounded the counter and stood before us.

"Just like that?" Rory asked, looking her over.

She was quite tall now that she was eye to eye. Her black flowery dress hung above her knees and her black, laced, heeled boots went almost halfway up her shins. I liked her style. In fact, I liked her quite a lot and she was still a stranger.

Sage looked at me as if she knew that I knew things with a certain knowing. *What a mouthful.*

"You can wait at *Molly McCreedy's*," the Witch told us. She pointed across the street. "I'll fetch ma. It won't take long."

"You're not worried about us?" Rory asked, glancing at me.

A smile spread across her face. "No."

There was something she wasn't telling us and I realised Derrydun wasn't as empty as we thought it was. It didn't matter. I knew the power I held couldn't be contained by any means, let alone Witch magic.

"Okay," I said. "We'll wait in the pub."

3
———

"Are you sure about this?" Rory asked as we crossed the road.

"Yes."

I looked up at the pub and decided I liked it. The building itself was something out of the Middle Ages. The whitewashed walls were covered in a thick layer of vines, and the exposed beams had been painted black. A sign hung near the door and pictured a woman in a dress and a fancy up-do. I assumed this was Molly McCreedy herself.

"They're just cautious," I added. "You would be too if a couple of unknown supernaturals turned up on your doorstep."

Rory sighed. I could tell he was on edge, but we had no say here. The Crescents would either allow us to go through the portal or they would turn us away. It was that simple.

Pushing open the door of the pub, I was

immediately hit with the scents of wood smoke, stale beer, and cooking.

Stepping across the threshold, I glanced around with interest. It looked like a photo inside a tourist brochure that proclaimed it as *the* traditional Irish pub people had to put on their must-see list… or they're not doing Ireland right.

The ceiling was low and crooked, but it didn't stop the owners from cramming the walls full of framed photos and paintings, all mismatched. A large portrait hung over the bar itself, picturing the same woman on the sign outside. The golden frame had a plaque set into the bottom reading 'Molly McCreedy — 1655-1687'.

Behind the rich, mahogany bar were three shelves stacked high with bottles, most of them full of whiskey, and below that were glass-fronted fridges stacked with cans of larger bottles of craft beer and other mixed drinks.

An open fireplace sat cold and empty at the opposite end of the room, the dark mouth covered with a wrought iron grate, and a bright landscape painting hung over the mantle. It looked like a contemporary impression of the village, complete with the main road, hot pink cottage, and the ruins on the hill. A veil of magic sat layered over the top of the brushstrokes and I squinted, trying to make it out. It wasn't Colour or Fae power, but something else… *witch magic.*

"I wouldn't look too closely at that if I were you,"

a woman behind the bar said. She looked me over, studying my green hair before glancing at Rory. "It has a bad habit of trying to hypnotise people."

"Then why hang it in the pub?" Rory asked.

"We hang it there so were can keep an eye on her." The woman winked. "So, what can I get you?"

"We're just waiting for someone," I said.

"Ah, I see. Pull up a stool then. The first drink is on the house."

"Cider?" I asked uncertainly.

"You got it." The woman looked at Rory.

"Beer. Whatever."

"Whatever?" She raised an eyebrow and grabbed a pint glass. "That's a dangerous order to give a bartender." Pulling a golden tap down, she began to fill the glass. "But I've got a good eye, so I'm sure I'll find something you'll like."

"You're supernatural, Maggie," the man at the end of the bar said, raising his glass.

The woman, Maggie, gave us a wink. "Not quite. I just know people. It's a skill learned from being behind a bar for the past thirty years." She set down two coasters in front of us and set our pints on them. "There you go. Don't drink them all at once." Then she picked up a tea towel and wiped her hands, before disappearing out back.

It seemed to be a signal of some kind, because at that moment, the outside door opened, letting in a beam of sunlight. A woman who looked like an older version of Sage strode in and the door crashed closed like an exclamation point announcing her arrival. Her gaze found us, and she smiled.

At that moment, Ignis wriggled in my bag and with a great deal of fuss, worked his way out, morphing from a kitten into a fully grown cat in the blink of an eye. Shaking himself, he prowled across the bar like he owned the place.

"*Ignis*," I hissed, but he didn't seem fazed at all about his surroundings, or the people gawking at him.

The man at the opposite end looked up from his pint and watched the cat with wide eyes, but the look the woman gave him was next level.

"Oh, my goodness," the newcomer murmured. "A magical cat. What is it with tabbies?"

"Excuse me?" I asked.

"Don't get me wrong," she went on, "I love cats. My husband is one from time to time, and Father O'Donegal used to have one that prowled around the church and slept on the altar. I distinctly remember him sitting there and licking his private parts during my mother's funeral. When he died, we had him immortalised in bronze. Not literally, of course… that would be classified as animal cruelty."

"*Tha a ceann anns a 'bhrochan*," Rory muttered.

"I can understand you, you know," the woman said.

I glanced nervously at Rory. "Uh, this is not quite what we were expecting."

The woman raised her eyebrows. "It never is."

I coughed nervously. "Are you…"

"Skye Williams," she declared, looking us over. "I'm the matriarch of the Crescents. If you have anything to say, I'm the one to say it to. Now, who are you and *what* are you?"

"I'm Elspeth, and this is Rory."

Her gaze lingered on me. "*Hmm.* Elspeth with the green hair."

"You're Australian," I blurted.

"And so are you, by that accent." She pulled up a stool and sat beside me. "So, how does a Fae end up all the way down there, so far away from the portals, huh? Care to share?"

"Well… I'm not exactly Fae. I am, but I'm not all the way Fae."

Rory snorted. "She's half."

"Half of what you are," Skye declared. "Which is?"

"Druid," he fired back. "We're Druids."

The Witch stared at us for a moment, clearly thrown by his response. Whatever she was expecting us to say, it wasn't that.

"Druids?" She looked thoughtful for a moment. "We've seen their marks in the forests, but they are ancient… There's caves, too."

"Fake Druids, you mean," Rory huffed, clearly offended. "They make their wee caves out of boulders and draw their runes in the mud, but they hold no power. Charlatans, the lot of them. *Fàidhean meallta.* Humans."

Skye looked at Ignis, who was sitting at the other

end of the bar, dipping a paw into the man's pint of beer. She chuckled before turning back to us. "Well, that explains how you were able to live so far away. You don't need a connection to maintain your luscious green hair."

"It wasn't always green," I said.

Rory cursed in Gaelic. "She doesn't even know what they did…"

I elbowed him. "Rory. *Please*."

"She's joking about your *hair*."

"How would they know about us?" I hissed. "Until I came along, all you did was hide in the Warren."

"Know what?" Skye asked, loudly. "I am sitting right here. I'm only fifty, not five million. I've also got all my teeth, twenty-twenty vision, and stellar hearing."

"And a temper sent straight from hell," the man called out, swatting Ignis away from his pint.

"Shut your pie hole, Sean McKinnon!" Sky bellowed. "Or I'll tell them about the time you were drunk on the roof singing *My Heart Will Go On* by Celine Dion!"

"That's low, even for you!" he cried.

"Can you believe this lot? They fight worse than a pack of toddlers," Rory said to me. "They'll never let us near their portal, let alone apologise for giving power to the Chimera. We should have tried it the old-fashioned way."

"No," I declared, turning my back on Skye as she

argued with the man known as Sean McKinnon. "The last time you opened a portal, a hellhound from another world almost ate us all. We only just got here."

"What's this about a hellhound?" Skye asked, tapping me on the shoulder. "And the bit about portals? And did you say… Chimera?"

Rory stood, his expression turning dark. "Aye, I said Chimera. A Dark Fae doomsday cult with a fixation on our people. They've hunted us for *twenty-five years*."

Skye swallowed hard. "Oh dear."

"They wanted to take us, strip our powers, and—"

"*Rory*," I snapped.

"He's angry," Skye told me. "Let him get it out."

"They killed my parents. They killed my best friend's mother and more besides. They took our home away from us, forcing us underground like pathetic worms. They would never have held any power here, but you had to open your precious portal."

The pub door opened again and this time, a man entered. He was handsome to look at, even though he was old enough to be my father. He stood tall with strong shoulders, stubbled jaw, and dark hair with a dusting of grey at his temples. A red- and black-checked shirt, jeans, and work boots completed his Irish farmer ensemble.

When he saw Rory all up in Skye's face, he strode over. "I think that's enough," he said, pressing his palm against the Druid's chest. "I know you're angry, but it seems we didn't even know you were in the world."

Rory scoffed. "What do you know? You just walked in."

"He flew in earlier," I said, watching the man. "It's nice to put a face to the falcon."

This statement seemed to diffuse the situation and Rory stared at me.

"This is Boone, my husband," Skye told us. "Witch, shapeshifter, sometimes tabby cat, sometimes—"

"Gyrfalcon, actually," Boone said, smiling at me. "You've got a good eye."

"You'll have to forgive Rory here," I went on. "We've been through a war because of the Chimera, so there's a little animosity amongst the Druids because of your portal. It's also a very long story."

"The Fae are supposed to remain in Ireland," Skye said. "If they're travelling beyond, then it's not sanctioned."

"And we definitely didn't know about it," Boone added.

It was probably because the Fae who lived in Edinburgh and elsewhere were exiles. It wasn't just Yenris'del who was forced to linger in alternate places of power in order to survive. Whoever their queen was, she wasn't absolute, at least not on Earth.

"Besides," Skye went on, "the farther they get from the portal, the weaker they are."

"Are you saying we're weak?" Rory demanded.

"Not at all. We've heard of the Chimera and their power, but we had no idea they had an operation here on Earth."

"So why were they after you?" Boone wondered.

"He said something about their portals," Skye mused, "didn't you?"

"I think we better leave it at that for now," Rory said. "At least until you offer us some reassurance that you're not just like them."

Skye snorted and looked to Boone. "Just like them?" To us, she said, "The Fae in Ireland used to hunt witches for their magic. *Our magic.* They couldn't survive without the portals being open, so when they were cut off, they sucked us dry for a thousand years."

"Until Skye put an end to it," Boone stated.

"Why did the portals close in the first place?" I asked.

Skye eyeballed me and used my same words I had given her. "That's a very long story."

I quite liked her—as I did her daughter—and sensed nothing malicious in her speech, so I stared back and said, "Seems to be a lot of that going around lately."

She glanced at Rory.

"We've been through a lot quite recently," I explained. "A week ago, we fought the Chimera in Scotland. We won, and they're finally gone from the Earth, but it was a difficult fight."

"And now you come to us," Skye said. "So, Elspeth Odhweine, why are you here?"

There was no harm in telling her. The truth was the best way to make them understand that we only wanted what was best for the Earth and the Fae beyond.

"I never knew my Fae mother or the world I came from," I told them. "I need to know what became of her… and learn what it truly means to be Fae."

Skye smiled, her hand reaching for Ignis. I could tell by the way she held herself that she knew there was much more to the story but didn't intend to press. Not yet, anyway.

Ignis allowed her to stroke his fur, his prisms glittering as her magic brushed up against them.

"Say…" she declared after a moment, "are you hungry?"

Rory and I looked at one another.

"She's inviting you over for dinner," Boone said with a chuckle.

The Witch sighed. "I'm not doing the cooking, so no need to worry."

"After all this time, all she can do is press buttons on a microwave."

Skye shrugged and grinned at us. "So?"

I turned to Rory, who's expression was unreadable. I wondered if he felt better after getting out his anger over the portals.

"We'll give you a minute to decide," Skye said, rising from the stool. "We'll wait for you outside."

I didn't speak until they'd gone. Noticing Maggie the bartender had made herself scarce, and Sean McKinnon was asleep at the bar, I didn't feel bad about speaking openly.

"We can trust them," I said to Rory. "It's why we came here."

"I didn't expect it to be so difficult," he replied. "Seeing them so oblivious to what they've done…"

"They had their own struggles." I glanced at the painting. "The Fae wanted to possess their power, too."

"Not in the same way."

I sighed. "No, not in the same way."

"You didn't tell them about…" he trailed off, and wisely so. The black sun wasn't the easiest thing to explain and would likely change the Crescent's warm welcome to something a little frostier.

"She knows I'm not telling her everything," I said, "but revealing that is the last thing I want to do."

"So you want to go to dinner with them instead?"

"They're inviting us into their home, Rory. They don't seem the type to twist this into a trap." I tapped my forehead. "I know things… I can sense their goodness."

"If you say so." The Druid sighed and glanced at the sleeping human at the end of the bar. Ignis had resumed dipping his paw into the now unsupervised beer.

"Ignis," I called. "Time to go."

He hopped off the bar and sauntered over to the door and waited for us.

"We have no choice," I said to Rory. "I'm hungry."

I scooped up my bag and made for the door. Behind me, I heard Rory sigh for the millionth time, then his boots stomped on the rickety floorboards as he came after me.

I guess he was hungry, too.

4
———

Needless to say, the matriarch of the Crescent Witches was not who we were expecting to meet.

We walked with Skye and Boone across the street, past *Irish Moon*, and down a path beside the shop. Directly behind was a garden full of flowers, herbs, and vegetables. A quaint, two-storey, stone cottage emerged from amidst the greenery, and I liked it immediately.

It looked like something out of a fairytale —*Goldilocks and the Three Bears* came to mind—and I looked for the Big Bad Wolf in the forest beyond.

"Do you like it?" Skye asked, seeing the wonder on my face.

I nodded. "It's very homely."

"It's a few hundred years old, at least. Been in the family since it was built."

They led us up the path to the cottage, Boone

jangling a set of old-fashioned iron keys. The lock clicked and clanked, and the moment the door cracked open, Ignis took off, shimmying through the gap and into the cottage, likely lured by the smell of food wafting outside.

"Sorry," I said, my shoulders sinking. "He doesn't seem to understand personal boundaries."

They laughed and told us not to worry about it.

Inside, Skye turned, blocking the threshold. "Oh, before I forget, we leave the giant knives in the hallway," she told us with a smile. "They'll be quite safe by the umbrellas."

I glanced at Rory before turning back to Skye. "How did you know?"

"We may go about our magic in different ways, but I don't think we're so different at our cores."

Rory shrugged, resigned to the fact that we were well and truly in this now, and unhooked his knife from his belt. I did the same, studying the photographs hanging on the wall.

A brass frame pulled my attention, the picture inside a haunting capture of two girls holding hands in a wild forest, their long hair frizzy and flowing. I recognised the black-haired girl as Sage, but the blonde was an enigma. She looked like Sage, but her hair was white as ivory.

"That's Sage and Hazel when they were thirteen," Skye explained.

"You have another daughter?" Rory asked.

"She lives away," Skye replied. "Sage and Hazel are identical twins. They're Geminis."

I didn't know what that was, so I just smiled and nodded.

Skye didn't seem to notice. "Sage lives in Boone's old cottage on the other side of the village. I asked her to come for dinner, but she rarely listens to her poor mother these days." She sniffed dramatically. "They grow up so fast."

"We're the same age, I think," I stated.

"It's too bad you're not going to be staying long, then. She could do with some company. Now, what does your cat like to eat?" she called out as she moved into the kitchen.

"Ignis," I said. "His name is Ignis."

"Ignis," she said, testing the word out. "Strong. I like it."

"He'll eat anything, but he doesn't need food."

"What is he exactly?"

"He's a construct," I explained, lingering in the hallway. "My grandmother made him out of prisms. Colour."

"Colour?" She stuck her head through the door. "Is that what you call your magic?"

I nodded. "She caught his shattered human soul on the edges of death and saved him."

"Really?"

"Yes. He has a few memories of his life before, but he can't vocalise them. He showed them to me in visions."

"You're telling them an awful lot," Rory muttered.

"They're our friends," I told him. "I don't mind."

"You seem sure of that," Skye noted.

I shrugged. "I *know* things… sometimes."

"Interesting." She waved us into the kitchen. "Come inside and take a seat. Our home is open."

I stepped into the kitchen, the smell of cooking stronger in here. Dried herbs hung from the ceiling, reminding me of Osna's workroom in the Warren, and various pots and pans took up the remaining room on the walls. Another rickety door led out to the side garden, and the lace curtains—tinged brown with age—hung over the windows.

Boone leaned against the counter while an older woman with frizzy grey hair fussed over a cutting board. She hastily stabbed at a pile of carrots, chopping unevenly.

Skye laughed at the sight of her so worked up and turned to us. "This is my mother, Aileen."

"I thought you said she was dead," Rory stated.

"Not quite," the elder woman told him and turned around. "They buried me and everything. I hear it was quite the affair."

"The hole was empty," Skye said with a huff.

"I was buried alive by a Spriggan," Aileen said to us, using the knife to gesture. "Same thing, really."

I stared at them. "A… what?"

They seemed taken aback at my lack of knowledge and glanced between one another.

"Oh dear," Aileen muttered, setting down the knife.

"A Spriggan is a spirit of the forest," Skye explained. "They are also tricksters who can change their face, appearing human one moment and tree-like the next."

I swallowed hard. I knew travelling to the Fae world was going to be hard, but the reality was beginning to set in.

"What... what other things are there?" I asked uneasily.

"Don't worry, Elspeth," Aileen said, revealing she already knew more about us than we did her. "Most Fae are humanoid, like us and you. They have their own magic and customs, but there are also other humanoid and elemental people. The Spriggans are but one earth elemental species. There are sprites, spirits, goblins—"

"*Mum,*" Skye scolded and turned to me with a reassuring smile. "It's not all that scary. There is plenty of good there, just as there is here. Life isn't that different when you drill down. They're just more open about the existence of magic than we are on Earth."

"Medieval hippies," Boone said with a chuckle. "That's the best way to describe them."

Skye cursed at him in Gaelic, the Irish lit more musical than the harder Scots I was used to.

"What about those who hold power?" Rory asked. "Their queen..."

"The Crescents have a tentative alliance with the Queen of the Fae, Niarisshia," Skye explained. "We may have done them a favour by defeating Carman and allowing their people to return home, but they are a secretive and flighty lot. They don't trust easily."

"Carman?" I asked, glancing between the Witches.

Boone frowned and Skye placed a hand on his arm. I watched the silent exchange closely. Something bad had gone down, and I was beginning to feel awful about all the negative things I'd thought about the Witches. I didn't know them, and they had their own stuff to deal with. The Druids weren't an island anymore.

Boone rose and began fussing in the fridge, taking out a jug of fruit juice.

"Carman is an ancient Witch," Aileen explained. "She was banished from Ireland a long time ago but managed to find her way back by syphoning the magic out of any Witch she could lay her hands on. The Covens went into hiding and a lot of us lost our lives. It was a mess that almost led to our extinction."

Extinction. I squirmed, smiling to cover up my uneasiness as Boone set glasses of juice before me and Rory.

"What did she want?" Rory asked.

"Ultimate power," the older Witch replied with a shrug. "It's what all evil wants… the power to dominate. Carman wanted to break open the portals and take over the Fae realm, but Skye was here to stop her."

"So the portals were closed to stop Carman," I said, voicing my thoughts. "And reopened once the danger had passed."

"To allow the Fae trapped here to go home," Skye told me. "One portal remains as a bridge between worlds—literally and figuratively."

I tensed at her words, the echo of the prophecy hanging over my head, almost crashing down on me.

"Crossing is one thing, but you'll have to present yourself to Queen Niarisshia," Skye went on. "She'll know if a new supernatural creature passes through the portal."

"We can speak to Ambassador Elmarrin. He might be willing to present you," Boone added.

Rory nodded. "We want to make a good impression. We aren't up to speed on their customs. Insulting their queen is the last thing we want to do."

I added my agreement with a sharp nod. I may not be welcome being who I was, but with an introduction, at least we'd get a foot in the door.

"Elmarrin can be a bit eccentric, but he's a good guy," Skye said. "Boone will fetch him in the morning. For now, you're welcome to stay here for the night."

"I'm making a hearty Irish stew," Aileen said proudly.

"It smells lovely," I told her.

"Have you any bags?" Skye asked. "Boone can go help you get them while dinner cooks, Rory."

I glanced at the shapeshifter. Skye sure ordered him around a lot. I must have my thoughts plastered on my face because he grimaced.

Boone raised his eyebrows. "Happy wife, happy life, am I right?"

The Crescent's guest room was a quaint little bedroom with a wrought iron, queen-sized bed topped with a pink patchwork quilt and matching tapestry cushions. It also smelled like a potpourri bomb had gone off.

Ignis had made himself scarce, disappearing into the forest around the village to explore. I wasn't worried about him; the cat could take care of himself and then some. He'd appear again when he was ready.

I stared at the powder-puff pink bed while Rory peered through the curtains and out the window. There wasn't a couch or another mattress hidden underneath, which meant…

Rory caught me staring and snorted. I flushed and looked away, busying myself with my backpack. The Crescents thought we were *together*, together.

"We're adults, Elspeth," he said, trying to hide his amusement. "We can sleep in the same bed."

"Shut up," I hissed. "I know I'm awkward. Just… leave it be."

"They seem decent," Rory said, his voice slightly muffled as he took off his jumper.

I glanced over my shoulder, flushing again as I caught sight of Rory's bare back. I hadn't seen him without his shirt on before and I was oddly transfixed. I had to get out more.

"You know that painting in the pub?" he asked.

"What about it?"

"It's a prison world," he murmured, giving me a look like it was a great secret. "I think they trapped that Carman Witch in there."

"How do you know? Did Boone tell you?"

"He didn't have to. Did you see the way he reacted when you asked about her? Something's going on there."

"Yes, but it's not our place to gossip about it," I told him. "We're here for the portal."

He shrugged and dropped his trousers.

I slapped my hands over my eyes. "Rory!"

"What? I like to sleep in my underpants. Do you want the left or right?"

"*Not helping.*"

He laughed. "I'm talking about the bed, not my balls."

I sighed and rolled my eyes. "Turn around."

"Why?"

I threw a pillow at him and he turned around while I changed into the old T-shirt I liked to sleep in. Finally, I stood at the edge of the bed, but something held me back.

"Rory?"

"Hmm?" He glanced over his shoulder, his eyes sparkling in the lamplight.

"Are we doing the right thing?"

"You're asking *now*?"

"I'm just worried, I guess."

"You've got nothing to worry about," he told me. "You're strong, Elspeth. Fearless. You've faced Chimera, walked through death, and then some. Believe in yourself, because everyone else believes in you."

I lowered my gaze. "I guess you're right, but I'm not fearless."

"Just in the face of danger."

A peel of laughter escaped my lips and I slid into bed. Rory rolled underneath the blankets, pressed his cheek against the pillow, and stared at me.

"What?" I whispered, not daring to look at him.

"We'll be okay," he replied. "Niarisshia may be a queen, but she's just a Fae. If she has any heart, she'll listen to us. She may not have answers, but permission to look for them is the next best thing."

"What if she doesn't want to help us?"

"That's a bridge we'll cross when we come to it." He rolled over and turned off the lamp, plunging the room into silvery shadow.

I stared at the unfamiliar ceiling and hoped he was right.

"Rory?" I whispered.

"Hmm?" came his muffled voice in the darkness.

"Thank you."

He raise this head. "For?"

"Coming with me. After everything I put the Druids through…"

"Don't mention it," he told me. "I wouldn't miss this for the world."

5

———

After a hearty breakfast the next morning, served again by a frazzled Aileen, Skye dragged me outside, excited to show me the village of Derrydun.

I reached out to Rory with wide eyes, but she was too overbearing, and I was out the door and in the garden before I could take a breath. All the Druid could do was shrug as Boone began to pepper him with questions about the goings-on in Scotland.

Ignis appeared from underneath a pumpkin leaf, leaping into step with us. He purred happily, prancing like a pony competing in a dressage championship.

"Where are we going?" I asked as the Witch guided me away from the main road and down a worn path.

"I want to show you something," Skye replied. "And have a little girl time. I love Boone, don't get me wrong, he looks devilishly handsome when he decides to be a horse, but sometimes the testosterone is too much for me to handle. Especially in stallion form." She raised her eyebrows. "Am I right?"

I snorted, clapping a hand over my mouth to stifle my laughter.

Sky smirked. "I'm so right. Men are men, no matter what supernatural race they come from."

"Rory certainly thinks he can do everything on his own," I said.

"What is it with you two? Are you a couple?"

I shook my head. "We're just friends."

"Just friends?"

I felt my cheeks heat and thought about Vanora… and the black sun. "It's complicated."

Sky chuckled and shook her head, letting the topic slide. *Thank goodness.*

The forest thickened the farther along the path we ventured, and soon the village seemed like it was a million miles away. The clamour of birds chirping in the trees filled the air as the breeze rustled leaves overhead. Cracking branches and other unfamiliar wilderness sounds echoed from far away, and I looked around, feeling slightly on edge. I knew it was only my mind playing tricks on me, but the landscape seemed alive with eyes.

"Do many Fae come here?" I asked. "It seems quiet."

"Sometimes," Skye told me. "Earth isn't a place where many choose to remain. The Fae who became trapped suffered a great deal and were glad to return, though some came back."

"Because they'd lost their identity?" I mused.

"Exactly. A thousand years is a long time, even to the Fae."

"What exactly do you do here, then?"

"The Crescents keep the peace," she explained. "Unfortunately, there is still some animosity between the Covens and the Fae. Not all are willing to let bygones be bygones, if you know what I mean. Consider us the supernatural Customs and Border Protection Agency."

"I get it. After so much suffering, it's hard to let go."

Skye regarded me for a moment, her expression closed. I brushed my green hair behind my ear and began to fidget. She definitely had a presence and knew how to exert it, that was for sure.

"I was like you once," she mused when she'd found what she was looking for. "I didn't know I was a Witch until my birthright called me here. I was on my own, except for Boone, and had to figure things out the hard way. I made mistakes and caused trouble through my ignorance, but that's how I learned. You had a whole people who disliked you from the start... except for that Rory of yours. Am I right?"

"How did you know?"

Skye smiled. "Let's just say it was an educated guess."

As far as rapport building went, Skye was a

master. She knew I liked her, and knew I'd eventually tell her everything she wanted to know, but not in a malicious way. Skye Williams cared about people.

It wasn't long before a clearing opened in front of us, the forest parting to allow us into the presence of a power that made my knees weaken.

The hawthorn tree stood out amongst the bright emerald, its leaves and trunk darker, but it was its size that had me awestruck at first.

Short and squat, the gnarled tree barely stood above the canopy of the rest of the forest, but its trunk had a girth that would need five or six people to encircle it with arms outstretched. Its branches wove a thick pattern that hung over the clearing, protecting all that stood beneath. It was as if someone had flung a warm blanket over us, soothing all the pain and worry out of my bones. *Magic*.

It wasn't like *Salle*, who was mostly grown with Colour, but this was right up there.

"I can feel it," I whispered, staring up at the tree.

The branches twisted with invisible fire the stretched into every leaf, twig, and scrap of bark. Power flowed into the roots, pouring energy into the earth itself, pooling into the clearing and beyond. If I focused on it, I was sure it would stretch right underneath Derrydun.

That's why this place was ground zero for the one and only portal between worlds.

"It's been here for thousands of years," Skye said, smiling up at the tree. "It's lived longer than Witches or Fae. And even longer than humanity." She pointed to a hollow at the base of the thick trunk. "The portal is down there."

I followed her finger and studied the dip between the roots. It was large enough for someone to descend, and I wondered if it looked like the portals the Druids opened.

"Who made the them?" I asked. "Do you know?"

Skye shook her head as Ignis prowled around the base, sniffing and pawing at the earth. "They've been here for thousands of years. How many exactly, no one knows. Maybe they grew with the saplings, or maybe someone created them. There is no proof either way."

"Are they all under hawthorn trees?"

"Yes. Hawthorns carry power. They shelter words and magic, which make them perfect guardians. Their roots travel deep." She placed her hand on the trunk and smiled. "All the other portals are sealed. This is the only one open."

"It's beautiful."

"Isn't she?" Skye turned, and looked me over. "I'll show you mine, if you show me yours."

I blinked. "Excuse me?"

She lifted her hands and the leaf litter began to stir, then lifted gently off the ground like delicate feathers buffeted by the wind. Golden light shimmered in the clearing, an effect from her magic that I wasn't sure she could see.

I spun around in wonder, watching the leaves

hover. Some spun in circles, others fluttered, but they all remained in place carried by Skye's golden magic.

"Cool, huh?" The Witch laughed then lowered her hands. The leaves fell back into place, settling as if they'd never moved to begin with.

"What else can you do?" I asked, curious.

"Nuh-uh," she said with a *tsk*. "Your turn."

I looked down at my hands, my heartbeat speeding up. The icy tendrils of the veil brushed against my fingers and I curled them into tight fists. Pushing death away, I called on my Colour. Opening my palm, I gathered a tendril of holographic thread and began to weave.

A line formed, growing into two, sprouting angles and curves, glittering and pulsing before it flared as the prism took shape—a single, red rose bud.

I looked up at Skye and held out the flower. The Witch plucked it from my fingers and twirled it around, studying every facet with keen eyes.

"Remarkable," she murmured. "It feels real."

"Ignis is made from the same power," I said, glancing at the cat, who'd climbed up into the hawthorn. I called for him to get down, but Skye waved a hand at me.

"He's fine. Let him climb." She held the rose out to me. "Here."

Taking it from her, I held the stem between my thumb and forefinger. I opened myself up to the prism again and the threads unravelled. The rose dissolved, falling in on itself, splintering like shards of crystal, and the Colour returned to where it'd come from.

"Druid Colour," Skye mused. "The threads of nature." Her smile widened. "We share the same beliefs. That's good to know."

"We would be friends, but I don't speak for the Druids," I said. "There's only so much I can tell."

"I understand. Perhaps I can meet your leaders one day."

"Well, this is the first step."

"We have done your people a great disservice, but you must know it wasn't personal."

"You didn't know we existed," I told her. "The Druids are like that. Even before they came to Earth, they were a wary and secretive lot."

She studied me for a moment. "You speak of them like you are an outsider."

"They're my family, but…"

"You're not full-blooded. I see."

"It's not like that exactly. I…" I sighed. "Actually, it was exactly like that."

Skye smiled and placed her hand on my shoulder. "They were hunted by the Chimera. They were hurt and needed something to blame." She glanced at the path we'd walked along. "Like your friend Rory needed to blame me for your misfortune. It wasn't personal."

"Circumstance," I said. "It was just circumstance."

"Actions can have unintended consequences.

Choices ripple outward with no telling where they will travel."

"You would totally get along with my grandmother Delilah," I said with a chuckle.

"Things are okay with you now?"

I nodded. "They're my family. We fought together at the end."

"I'm glad to hear it. Now," she said, "do you think it's time to tell me about the other reason you want to go through the portal?"

I flushed and looked at my feet. What if I revealed the truth and she turned me away? My powers were dangerous and in the wrong hands… I wanted to go to a world where the Chimera were still active and much more powerful than they'd been here on Earth. I was one giant risk wrapped up in a doomsday prophecy.

"You can trust me, Elspeth," she murmured. "I know we just met, but the Crescent Witches are here to foster peace. We fight, but only when necessary."

I swallowed hard. *What if I was necessary?*

"The Chimera," I began slowly. "They didn't just come after the Druids for their power…"

Skye's expression became troubled. "They wanted you."

I nodded. "I can… I can do things they want. My mother had power they needed and with my Colour…" I trailed off uneasily.

"The Druids can open portals of their own."

My panicked gaze found hers.

"Don't worry, Elspeth," she said, placing her hands on my shoulders. "I'm not here to judge you. I'm here to help. I'd be a terrible guardian if I didn't ask the hard questions."

"I…" I swallowed the lump in my throat. "I come with a prophecy. One the Chimera believe will deliver them absolute power."

"I see."

"My Druid family is known for Spirit Walking," I went on. "Walking in death. I can go there, but…"

Skye tightened her grip on my shoulders, the pressure grounding me. "Your Fae power?"

"I can control the veil between life and death. I can change the currents that take souls away. I become…"

"Oh, dear." Skye sighed and pulled me against her chest, her hands stroking my emerald hair… just like a mother would.

"The Chimera want to turn me," I murmured. "Just like they tried with my mother."

"And your Druid magic makes you ten times more powerful."

"A bridge between worlds," I whispered, quoting my doomsday prophecy.

"I can understand why you want to cross now," Skye said. "Understanding what you are is just as important as understanding your identity."

I pulled away, my heart skipping a beat. "You aren't worried?"

"No. Should I be?"

"Everyone else is."

"Elspeth, if you wanted to cause harm, you would have already done so. Us Witches have tricks of our own, you know."

"Well, maybe you're okay with it, but the queen will probably be pissed once she knows the truth. I don't know what I'm going to say to her."

Skye bit her bottom lip, then glanced at the hawthorn. "If this goes as deep as I suspect it does, then Niarisshia already knows about you and the Chimera's end game. She's cunning and that's saying something considering she's Fae. She's definitely not like her mother, Aibell. She's a new ruler and has youthful ambition bordering on ruthlessness."

I rolled my eyes. *"Great."*

"Elspeth, you defeated the Chimera here on Earth. That's a good thing. I'd lead with that if I were you."

"Brownie points?"

She smiled. "Epic brownie points."

I wiped at a stray tear.

"A lot has changed in the Fae world since I first went there. They had been at war when the portals reopened, only recently finding peace between the factions of Seelie and Unseelie. It takes a long time for those animosities to go away, if they fade at all. I would be cautious revealing your true nature, and the same goes for Rory. The power to create portals is a desire all Fae long for."

I thought about my dad and all he'd been through. "I suppose every world has its politics."

"Oh," Skye said abruptly, blinking up at the hawthorn. "Your cat levelled up."

I looked up into the branches were Ignis lay, his tiger stripes shimmering blue. He stretched out his massive paws and yawned, showing us his pointy teeth. He was proud of himself again and began to preen.

"Yeah," I said, "he does that sometimes. Flexing is kind of his thing."

We laughed at Ignis, the tension lifting off my shoulders.

"C'mon, let's go back to the village," Skye said. "No doubt Boone's found Ambassador Elmarrin by now."

I hesitated. "Should I…"

"I'd leave out the doomsday part," she advised. "If you want to stop the Chimera once and for all, getting through the portal and to an audience with Niarisshia is the first step."

I didn't even ask her how she knew. Skye, like me, seemed to have a knowing all her own. Maybe she had her own prophecy once upon a time.

"Where are we going now?" I asked as she led the way down the path, away from the clearing.

"To the pub," Skye said. "It's where everything interesting happens in this place."

Ambassador Elmarrin turned out to be a tall, elfish man who unfortunately reminded me of Mindel. The Fae certainly had a style akin to something out of a Tolkien novel. Though where Mindel was dark, Elmarrin was fair and his clothes—a light grey suit with delicate cream pinstripe and a matching silver shirt—were a little more Earth appropriate.

"You know I don't like to come in here," he was saying. "It stinks like stale urine and the painting gives me a chill I won't be able to get rid of for *days*."

Rory sat at a table by the fireplace with Boone, both looking thoroughly exasperated as Elmarrin complained. He must have been at it for a while. No wonder Ignis had demanded to get inside my bag before we'd come in.

Molly McCreedy's was otherwise empty, the bartender and the regular customers had made themselves scarce. I couldn't blame them.

"Oh, calm yourself, Elmarrin," Skye declared, sitting across from him at the rickety table. "You won't have to look at it for long."

"And why is that?" he purred, his silver eyes sharpening as he focused on me. The Fae's tone changed dramatically as Rory tugged me into the chair beside him. "What do we have here, then?"

"This is Elspeth Odhweine," she told him. "And you've already met Rory. They want to cross and petition Queen Niarisshia."

Elmarrin peered at me, his Fae aura playing against his skin. He noticed my uneasiness and smiled.

"Druids return and bring a half-cast with them. *Interesting.*"

"Excuse me?" I declared, offended.

"Don't take offence, child," the ambassador said with a sigh. "That's what you are, is it not?"

"The Fae aren't known for their tact," Boone murmured to us.

"We dislike lies," Elmarrin said coolly. "Especially when they're used to flatter and cajole."

"Are you sure you want to go?" Rory whispered in my ear. "I'm not sure I can take much more of this."

"Elmarrin here is special," Skye said with a smirk. "There's a reason he was appointed as ambassador. He's the perfect Fae to guide you through the portal and to the capital, aren't you?"

The Fae straightened his posture and smiled. "Undoubtedly."

Boone sniggered, earning himself a kick underneath the table from Skye. They were mocking him, but the Fae didn't seem to notice.

Elmarrin regarded me. "And why do you want to see our queen, child?"

"I never knew my Fae mother, ambassador," I replied. "I wish to learn more about her and what it means to be Fae."

"*Half* Fae."

I bristled and gritted my teeth.

"Is that all?"

I hesitated. "Is there supposed to be more?"

Elmarrin snorted and glanced uneasily at the painting hanging over the fireplace.

"We're also representing the Druids of Earth," Rory said. "We would present ourselves to your queen in regards to… Fae activity in our city."

"Your city?"

"Edinburgh," Rory added. "Scotland."

"There are no Fae outside of Ireland," the ambassador stated. "It is forbidden."

"Tell that to the Chimera," the Druid said, narrowing his eyes.

"*Chimera?*" Elmarrin cried out and shot to his feet. "You said nothing of Chimera!"

"Calm down," Skye said with a roll of her eyes. "The Druids took care of them."

"I will not! Next you will tell me that the half-cast is Chimera offspring!"

"I am not!" It was my turn to rise, along with my anger. "How dare you! After everything we went through to clean up your mess!"

"*Our mess?*" Elmarrin waved his hands.

"You didn't even know the Chimera were on Earth," I told him. "We took care of them before they could strip us of our power and destroy our home. They are gone from this world, though through no shortage of suffering on our behalf. The least *you* can do is escort us through the portal and to the queen. What happens after that is none of your concern."

Elmarrin scoffed, his lips thin.

"She's going to do just fine, don't you think?"

Boone murmured to his wife, who nodded in agreement.

"It is my concern," the ambassador fired back. "Everything that happens in this world is my concern."

"Oh, for goodness sake," Skye declared. "Seriously, Elmarrin. You're such a drama queen."

His sliver eyes focused on the Witch. "You may be close with the queen, but I see right through you, *Skye Williams*."

Skye smiled sweetly up at him. "We've got the painting for another six months, but you can take it with you if you want."

The ambassador huffed and turned his icy stare onto me and Rory. "I will escort you," he said, "if only to get away from the *matriarch*." He flipped his silky blond hair over his shoulder and stalked out of the pub, his power crackling irritably around him.

Rory and I stared after him as Skye and Boone began to laugh hysterically. What in the world had we just witnessed?

"You're welcome," Skye declared. "Thank you for taking him off our hands."

"Won't that cause trouble with the queen?" I asked. "I mean—"

"Someone give that man a smartphone, a selfie stick, and an Instagram account," she added. "*Stat.* I hear they're casting for the new season of *Love Island*."

"Don't worry about us," Boone said. "Elmarrin is

here for a reason, and it's not because he's a joy to be around… in any world."

Rory chuckled and nudged me under the table. "A different kind of exile."

"Point is, you got your ticket and we got a holiday," Skye said. "We owe you one."

"How about lunch?" Boone stood and rounded the bar, fetching some menus. "Pick anything you like. It's on the house."

"You're always thinking about food," Skye told him.

Rory looked at me as Ignis poked his kitten head out of my bag. "I kind of like them," he whispered in my ear. "Is that wrong considering?"

I shook my head. "No. Not at all. I like them, too."

Skye leaned close and winked. "I like me, too."

6

———

E lmarrin was already waiting for us at the hawthorn when we arrived.

The portal was open, the base of the tree glistening with magic. The surface ripped with gentle waves, a rainbow of colour spreading across the blackness, just like the ones created by the Druids. It was a comfort to see some things were universal.

"They await us on the other side," Elmarrin stated pompously.

Skye and Boone stood beside me and Rory, with Sage and Aileen bringing up the rear. It was nice of them to see us off, but I knew it was partly because they wanted to make sure the ambassador left them in peace… at least, for a little while.

"You're welcome to stay with us anytime," Skye said to me and Rory. "We'd love to see you on your way back… if only to find out how things went with Niarisshia."

I nodded. "Is there anything else we should know?"

"Parting wisdom, eh?" She scratched her chin. "Show her the flowers. Fae *love* flowers."

Rory chuckled. "Flowers, noted."

"And they don't always say what they mean," Boone added.

"We've definitely got experience with that," I said wryly.

"Then you know the basics of how to handle an audience with the queen," Skye told us. "Flowers and mind games."

"Thank you," I told the Crescents, "for everything."

"You're welcome," the matriarch replied, scratching Ignis behind the ear as he poked his kitten head out of my bag. "Take care."

Rory urged me forwards, the portal rippling in anticipation. *This was it.* The moment we stepped through, we'd be in the Fae realm and closer to finding out about my mother and the Chimera. Another battle was about to begin, but this time, it would be a war of politics, not knives and magic.

I had to be ready.

I was ready.

Elmarrin rolled his eyes at us and walked through the portal. Rory went next, a mere step before me, then Ignis and I crossed.

The hawthorn blinked out of focus and the world shifted. A painful feeling of tearing twisted me to the side, then I landed in a heap, my hip jarring and my knife pressing awkwardly into my thigh. Luckily for me, it was sheathed.

Cursing, I rolled over and looked for Rory, but he was nowhere to be seen. I was sitting in the middle of a strange forest… *alone*. My bag was gone and with it, everything I'd been carrying. *Ignis*.

"Ignis?" I whispered, looking around fearfully. *"Ignis?"*

The trees rustled, the breeze carrying an unknown sickly-sweet scent. It looked like any other forest on Earth, save for the knowledge that I was in another world, one full of Fae, magic… and Chimera.

Clearly, I wasn't where I was supposed to be.

"Rory?" I called softly. "Elmarrin?"

No one replied.

For a moment, I thought about phasing, but quickly dismissed the idea. I didn't know where I was. I had no points of reference, and I didn't know what anything looked like. I wasn't going anywhere.

I stood and dusted off my jeans. My hip ached, but I ignored it, looking around the forest instead. Which way was I going to go? There had to be some signs of life around. Maybe a road or a town was nearby. I could ask for directions there.

A snapping sound echoed through the woods and my head whipped around. My senses flared and I knew I wasn't alone. I felt dull Fae energy radiating from the shadows and an image of the Spriggans Skye and Aileen had told me about, sprang to mind.

But it wasn't elemental tree tricksters.

Four Fae men emerged from the thick forest, their ratty brown clothes rustling as they moved. Dull brown eyes focused on me as they circled, their blades glinting in the dappled sunlight. Alarm bells began rising in the back of my mind and I held up my hands.

"Please," I said. "I'm lost. Can you help?"

One of the men sniggered and another said something, his words unknown.

Whoever these people were, they weren't Chimera. What they were though, were thugs. They had no intention of helping me... only harming.

I went for my knife, but the larger Fae raised his hand and struck me with the hilt of his blade. One of the men behind me said something in an unknown language, then he shouted in my face and pushed me violently.

I fell to my knees, dazed as my power rose and the veil crept closer. I began to panic as the black sun flared hotter than it ever had. Was it more powerful here? Of course, it was... I was in the Fae realm.

"Please. You don't understand," I rasped. If I let go, things were going to get real dark, real fast. "I don't want to hurt anyone."

The Fae in front of me laughed, then kicked my shoulder, the heel of his boot dug painfully into my flesh. I landed on my back, the black sun thrashing against my hold.

Let me go. Let me go. Let me go.

I wasn't going to let the first thing I did here be death. It would go down in history as the worst decision *ever*. Letting go of my power would alert every Chimera in existence of my arrival and I could only imagine what the queen would think. *Way to impress the powers-that-be, Elspeth.*

But maybe she would praise you for killing some common thieves, the black sun whispered in my ear. *You'd be simply taking out the trash.*

I thrust my hands into my hair. "Shut up!"

The Fae began to argue amongst themselves as I cowered, agitated over my reaction. Maybe they thought I was crazy and would leave me alone, then I wouldn't have to—

A dark blur leapt into the clearing and knocked one of the attackers down. The Fae scattered, crying out in alarm.

I breathed heavily, stuffing the black sun back into its box the best I could, and rose my head. The blur was a man… who appeared to be making short work of the Fae. One was already on the ground, holding his face in agony.

The unknown man struck another attacker on the back of the neck with his elbow, then kicked their feet out from underneath them, adding another body to the pile.

Three and four followed, blood pouring out of a broken nose and cut lips.

Finally, my rescuer bellowed at them in a strange, musical, language, kicking the nearest Fae in the ribs.

"Leishrilei de tuathade lei li delei'an ash!"

The attackers scrambled across the clearing, kicking up dirt and leaves in their haste to get away.

"Ash! Leishrilei!" His voice followed them through the woods.

I pressed my palm against my throbbing forehead, the black sun simmering as I squinted up at the man. He turned to me, his expression cold and unforgiving.

He wasn't a bit like the Fae I'd met. He had the same angular features and sharp-tipped ears, but he had a hardness about him that reminded me of Jaimie and the fragment of Ignis I'd seen in death. He wasn't just a hunter… this guy was a warrior.

His dirty brown hair fell to his shoulders and small plaits had been roughly woven at either side to keep it from falling into his eyes. It must have been done a long time ago because they'd matted into dreadlocks, the silver clasps barely visible through the tangle of hair. His chin was also covered in ragged stubble that did nothing to cover the ugly scar that cleaved his jaw. If he took a bath and combed his hair, maybe he'd be handsome… but smelling nice wouldn't do a thing to sweeten his sour scowl.

My gaze fell to the dead bird hanging from his belt—some kind of parrot with emerald and back feathers—then to the knife in his hand.

"What are you doing out here?" he asked in English, looking me over with exasperation. His silver eyes flashed, and I looked away.

"I don't know," I told him, picking leaves out of my hair.

"Fae around here don't take kindly to the Shri'danann, but you know that, don't you?"

His question was loaded with a thousand unknowns and I wasn't sure what to reveal about myself. It was clear I had no idea what I'd gotten myself into. He was testing me, and I couldn't lie my way out of this.

"I-I came from Ireland."

He snorted. "That explains everything."

"What's that supposed to mean?" I demanded.

"If you're as clueless as I suspect, then you won't get far. They'll come back the moment I'm gone and hang you up by the ankles and slit your throat."

"Why? What did I do?"

The Fae raised his eyebrows. "You exist."

A chill splintered through my body and I scrambled to my feet, the pain in my shoulder and side forgotten.

"Come," he ordered and began to walk away.

"Why should I follow you?" I demanded.

The Fae stopped and spun on his heel. He tapped a finger to a silver badge pinned to his cloak—an eight-pointed star.

I scowled. It meant something important, but I had no idea what.

"*Tuathade'shri,*" he stated, tapping the star again. "The seal of the queen." Then he turned and began to walk away again.

"What's your name?" I called.

He glanced over his shoulder. "Altrys."

He kept going, expecting me to follow on that alone.

"Don't you want to know mine?"

"*No.*"

<hr>

I didn't have any other choice but to follow Altrys through the forest.

The farther we went, the more my mind raced. It was probably best to keep my identity a secret, at least until I figured out how things were here, and who Altrys was. He could be anyone, regardless of him claiming he carried Niarisshia's seal of approval.

Being alone in the Fae world as a Druid and a master of death made me a target for the Chimera… and who knew what else. My ignorance would lead me into worse trouble than a small-time vigilante hate group.

Altrys led me to a small camp set up in a hollow, the ground low enough to hide it from prying eyes and shelter it from the elements. It wasn't much to look at—a campfire ringed with stones and a pile of leaves. A blanket and a brown leather bag were stuffed under a gnarled tree root, but other than that, there was nothing else here.

The Fae told me to sit as he busied himself. Parking my arse on the ground, I watched closely as he plucked the feathers from the strange bird and winced as he took out his knife and chopped and sliced at the carcass. I'd come from a world of supermarkets and plastic packaging. Seeing where food really came from was an alien sight.

I picked up a stray feather and twirled it around in my fingers. It had been a beautiful creature, all black and emerald, but I was hungry, and nature was a cruel mistress. No wonder the Druids were vegan.

Altrys lay the meat on a rock while he threaded pieces onto wooden skewers. When he was done, he set them over the fire, twirling them around until the meat was cooked and the sticks were blackened.

Finally, he handed me one. "Here. Eat."

I took it gingerly and sniffed. Smelt like chicken.

Altrys ate like it was his last meal, wolfing down the bird without a sideways glance at me. Grease dripped over his fingers and he wiped them on his trousers. I didn't know if it was comforting, knowing that all Fae weren't as highly strung and vain as Elmarrin and Mindel.

I nibbled at the meat, wondering about allergies and compatible digestive systems. In the end, I decided it was in my best interests to not offend Altrys, so I chewed and swallowed, discovering that it did taste like chicken.

"How did you come here?" the Fae asked, not looking at me.

"I came through the portal and for some reason, it spat me out here."

"Well, that's a problem."

I grunted.

"The portal leads to the capital," Altrys said, his silver eyes turning to me. "This isn't the capital."

"I may have grown up in a different world, but I'm not blind. Of course, this isn't the capital." I lowered the skewer and licked my lips. "Where are we exactly?"

"The Western Reaches," he replied. "Two thousand leagues northwest from where you were supposed to be."

My heart twisted. "And how long is a league exactly?"

"Twenty-seven furlongs." *Great. That didn't help at all.*

I groaned and pinched the bridge of my nose. However far it truly was, it seemed like a long way regardless of furlongs.

"So how do I get back?" I asked.

"Walk."

"Walk? What about the portals?"

"You really are from another world." Altrys shook his head in bewilderment. "Portals are forbidden, though it doesn't really matter. No one has that kind of power anymore."

"Why?"

"I'll take you to the main road in the morning," he said, ignoring me. "There ought to be a trader or caravan headed in the direction you need."

"What about you?"

"I have work to do."

"What kind of work?"

"Do you always ask this many questions?"

I flushed and looked at the fire. "Not usually." Above, the sky seemed to be darkening, but it could just be the forest or a cloud covering the sun. "How long *is* a day?"

"Our world is a copy of yours," he told me, "but things are different. The landmasses, the weather, the people, the air. But our place in the universe is the same."

I thought about the hellhound that escaped Rory's portal and the world of fire it'd come from. A slight variation in the evolution of a world could change a lot of things...even the length of a day.

Altrys didn't seem too concerned. Even if he did tell me, he'd probably answer with some vague measurement system that meant nothing. I wished I wore a watch, then I could do my own experiment.

There were some questions he could answer, though. It seemed sensible for me to ask them while someone was around to begrudgingly answer them... without wanting to hang me by the ankles from a tree.

"Altrys?"

He glared at me and I chose to ignore him this time.

"Who are the Shri'danann?"

"Do they teach you anything in Ireland?"

I shrugged.

"The Shri'danann are the Higher," he said.

"Higher?"

"The Higher Fae. The Elite. Those with magic."

I hesitated. "Those people back there… They attacked me because…"

"They are the De'ashlide. Not everyone in this world is fortunate enough to be born with magic. It fosters division and resentment."

"And exploitation and suffering."

De'ashlide… I recognised part of the name and it brought back memories of the elemental soldier. It had called me *Liash li Ashli. Ashli* was death. *Ashlide* mustn't have much difference. To be without magic was a kind of death for the Fae. No wonder they'd attacked me.

"I don't know what you were expecting, but every world has its terrors…" Altrys narrowed his eyes at me.

"What?" I bristled, my annoyance starting to match his.

"Your name."

"What about it?"

"*What is it?*"

"Elspeth."

His lips moved, sounding out my name silently. After a moment, he seemed satisfied.

"Who are you exactly," I asked. "Are you one of the Shri'danann?"

"Not quite," was his reply.

I waited. And waited…

"What does that mean?" I prodded.

He picked up a stick and poked at my boots. "Exactly what you think it means."

I kicked the stick away and he chuckled. I looked down at his boots, then to mine. They were completely different. Mine had been made by human technology in a factory somewhere. His were made by hand, stitched and cured over a long time.

"You're a little of both," I murmured. *Like me.* "Shri'danann and—"

"Elspeth."

I blinked, confused.

"Unusual name. It's not Fae."

"We do things differently where I come from," I said with a pout.

He looked me over. "Clearly."

"I got here thirty minutes ago. Cut me some slack."

Altrys grunted, perplexed by my statement. He scooped up his ratty brown blanket and threw it at me. To his amusement, it hit me in the face.

"What's your problem?"

"It gets cold at night." He poked a stick into the fire, stirring the coals. "You're going to need it."

I wrapped my fingers around the coarse fabric. "You're letting me stay?"

"I'm the queen's blade. Of course I'm letting you stay." He raised his eyebrows. "I took an oath."

I grimaced and looked into the fire. I was the one who wanted adventure… I just didn't expect to be camping in a hostile environment the first night.

"Don't look so sad," Altrys said. "You'll have plenty of time to tell me about this Ireland of yours. I hear there are strange creatures living there." He looked me over.

"*Hilarious.*"

The Fae laughed and turned to cook the rest of the bird meat. I didn't know who was worse—my rescuer or that pompous twat, Elmarrin.

It didn't matter. I was stuck with Altrys… for now at least.

I wrapped the blanket around my shoulders and watched him work.

"Thank you," I said.

Altrys glanced at me, his silver eyes regarding me with an unknown expression. He nodded once, then resumed his cooking.

7

―――――

A soft rapping echoed on the other side of my bedroom door.

"Els?"

"Go away!" I buried my face into my pillow, my snot and tears staining the purple cover.

"Els? It's Dad. Can I come in?"

I didn't reply, but he opened the door anyway. The mattress dipped beside me as he sat, and I couldn't hold onto my sobs anymore.

"Why don't they like me?"

"Because you're pretty and smart and they're not," he told me.

"No, I'm not."

"Yes, you are." He stroked my hair. "It's easier for some people to lash out at others rather than do the work to be better at something."

I sniffed. "It's mean."

"Yes, it is, but remember it's not about you, Els. Doubt,

resentment, and jealousy can be ugly emotions. They make people do ugly things."

"It's not my fault they're stupid," I raged.

"Maybe not, but we come from a place of privilege."

"Privilege?"

"It means we have certain advantages because of those who came before us, or the family we were born into, even the country and the colour of our skin. Some people aren't as fortunate and have to work twice as hard to achieve the same things that are easy for others."

"Renee Donovan tore up my English homework and flushed it down the toilet, then took video of me crying while I tried to get it out. She sent it to everyone, Dad! She's the biggest bully in school."

He leaned closer. "And why is that?"

I blinked, my tears already drying on my cheeks. "What?"

"Why is she a bully?"

My shoulder jerked and my eyes opened. Dull light clung to the forest, the first rays of dawn creeping through the chill. Altrys stood over me, his expression dour.

"Did you just kick me?" I demanded.

"You sleep like the dead," he said. "It's time to go."

I sat up and scraped the leaves out of my hair, scowling at the Fae's back as he dumped earth over the campfire.

He thought I was nothing more than a burden. To be fair, I hadn't given him any reason to think I could help him or protect myself. If I did, I'd reveal myself to be a Druid *and* the black sun, and I didn't know what he knew about me or my prophecy. I didn't dare bring up the Chimera.

I rubbed my cold nose and stood, folding up his ratty brown blanket. Sleeping on the ground wasn't exactly my idea of a good time, but nothing had happened during the night—no bugs, no rain, no midnight ambushes. I supposed anything was an improvement after yesterday.

Altrys took the blanket and fastened it to his pack, then gestured for me to follow. I walked behind him, keeping one eye on him and one on the shadows.

"Where are we going?" I asked after fifteen minutes of scrambling ungracefully through the thick woods. Altrys looked like he was stepping on clouds while I clawed through the mud.

"I have to stop at the village before I leave you at the road," he replied.

"Village?"

The trees parted then, giving me a glimpse of the land beyond. Dull sounds of civilisation ebbed over a fast-flowing stream and across a dale. I craned my neck, but I couldn't see anything. The bushes were too thick, but smoke rose from across the water. Beyond, a jagged mountain range towered over everything, the tips frosted with snow and ice.

I stared in awe, realising I hadn't landed far from people after all.

"Sit here and don't make a sound," Altrys said.

"If someone sees you, they'll know you're not from here."

"What are you going to do?"

His eyes narrowed. "Just wait."

I sat on a fallen log with a sigh. "Fine."

Altrys ghosted through the forest, and within the space of a single breath, I was alone. I hoped he was coming back and hadn't left me here to rot. The view was quite nice, but that was about it.

Listening to the sounds of the forest, I began to weigh my options. I didn't have anyone else to trust. I didn't know the world, the people, or the language. They seemed to speak English—at least, Altrys did—but I didn't have a clue what those other men were saying. I held a knowing from my Druid heritage that helped me with Gaelic, but it didn't seem to translate Fae.

There was also something that marked me as one of the Shri'danann—a Fae with magic. Was it my green hair? Altrys said he was half, and he was rather plain to look at—in a coloured hair way, not that he wasn't handsome underneath the grime—and so were those men who'd attacked me.

The cool tendrils of death brushed against the edges of my powers and I stared into the woods. Nothing stirred, but I could still feel something lingering just out of reach.

There were spirits here.

I had no clue who, or what, they were. Good, evil, middling… All I knew was they were not of the living.

My palms itched to reach out for the veil, but it wasn't my place. Just because I had the power didn't mean I could challenge nature and do whatever I wanted.

My heart leapt as a shadow peeled away from the forest and emerged before me.

Altrys carried a green cloth-wrapped parcel in his hands, oblivious to the near death experience he'd just treated me to.

"This is for you." He tossed the package at me, which I managed to catch before it smashed me in the face. "I had to guess your size."

"My… size?" I felt the lumpy parcel. *He'd bought me clothes*.

I undid the string and spread out the fabric, which turned out to be the outer layer of a cloak, much like the one he wore with a hood and silver clasp. Inside the folds was a soft, earthy-coloured tunic and a pair of trousers.

I looked down at my "But I like this jacket."

"It's just clothing," he stated. I opened my mouth, but he shook his head in warning. "It marks you as different. The stitching is all wrong."

"As different as my hair?"

His lips thinned.

"That's a Shri'danann thing, isn't it?" I prodded. "Green hair comes with magic."

He nodded.

"You know, where I come from, people colour their hair with dye."

"You don't think people have tried that here? Fae hair rejects dye."

I stared at him bewildered. "Really? Because I coloured my hair when I was thirteen and my dad went full psycho."

It was Altrys's turn to stare at me.

"What?"

"You'd be better off changing into those clothes and leaving your Irleand-ish ones buried in a hole."

"Irleand-ish?" I raised my eyebrows. "What about my boots?"

"Boots are costly, and no one looks at anyone's feet." He made a show of looking me over. "And no one will care about your feet, Elspeth from Ireland."

I scowled at him with as much force as I could muster. "Then turn around, pervert."

He laughed but turned to face the other direction, folding his arms over his chest.

I shucked off my jacket and jumper, eyeing Altrys. Cool air tickled my bare skin and I straightened my bra before sliding on the tunic.

"I saw something in the forest while you were gone," I told him as I dropped my jeans.

"Shadows," the Fae stated, not moving.

"It wasn't shadows." I shivered and shoved my feet through the legs of the trousers. The fabric was quite soft. "I felt power. A coldness."

"Coldness?" He glanced over his shoulder, but luckily for him, I was already rolling my socks back onto my feet.

"You have ghosts here. Spirits. Did you know?"

He frowned and his cockiness seemed to melt away.

"What *are* you doing here?" I asked, sitting on the log. "What's so important to the queen that you're out in the middle of nowhere?"

"I've been ordered not to say."

I sighed and tugged on my boots. "You never asked why I came here. You made a big song and dance about demanding what I was doing, but not once did you ask *why*."

Altrys remained as still as a statue, staring at me like I was completely see-through.

"I understand some things," I went on. "How there were Seelie and Unseelie. How everyone was united in the aftermath of the portals reopening. I also understand how that kind of animosity doesn't go away just because a queen orders it to." I tied my bootlaces, then looked up at Altrys. "Which one were you?"

"Seelie, not that it's any of your concern."

"Oh, I see. You carry a fancy silver badge that marks you as a know-it-all with infinite power." I fastened my belt around my waist and made sure my knife was within reach. "We have those on Earth, too."

"It's lucky you came here first," the Fae said. "If you speak to the queen like that—"

"I came to this world to find out about my mother and her family. She may or may not be dead, but I'm leaning towards dead so I don't wind up disappointed. I figure because of my green hair, she was one of the Shri'danann. As for Seelie or Unseelie, I wouldn't know. Someone who might be able to help me figure it out is the queen. I don't know much, but I do know that I'll need her blessing before I begin digging and I can't go to her empty-handed. If the portal spat me out here, it has to mean something." I raked my gaze over him, taking in his height, frame, and the knife at his hip and sword on his back.

"Are you finished?"

"Let me help," I said, rising to my feet. "I'm not just some silly girl from another world. I'm capable."

He raised his eyebrows. "And how could you help me? You know nothing of this world, the people or the customs. Can you even use that knife?"

I narrowed my eyes. "Care to find out?"

"Let it be known that you invited this."

His blow was sloppy. Clearly, he didn't think much of my ability, so I took full advantage.

I dodged his arm, rammed the heel of my boot against the side of his knee, then as he crumpled to the ground, I fisted my left hand in his hair and flipped my knife into my right, ending the display with the serrated blade to his throat.

"Let it be known that you invited this," I purred. I shoved him away and slid my knife back into its scabbard. I said a silent thanks to Vanora and her high-octane knife lessons.

Picking up the cloak, I threw it around my shoulders and fussed with the clasp.

Altrys stood, his silver eyes burning into me. I didn't dare meet his gaze for fear I'd lose the power I'd just gained.

"Why didn't you fight back?" he asked. "In the forest? Why?"

"I… It feels different here." My fingers fumbled with the unfamiliar clasp.

Altrys grunted and knocked my hands away, fixing the brooch for me. "You're weak."

"Excuse me?" I demanded, jerking back. "I am not!"

"It's the truth. Fae do not lie."

"Oh, you so do," I scoffed.

"Sometimes. But it's easier to tell the truth. You're weak. Afraid. You could have real power here, Elspeth from Ireland, but you're too weak to accept who you really are."

He had no idea.

"You're such an arsehole," I hissed.

"Arsehole?" His brow furrowed. "What is this?"

I slapped him on the butt cheek with the flat of my knife and he flinched. "That's your arse. It doesn't take a genius to figure out where the hole is."

Altrys stared at me for a moment, then burst out into peals of laughter.

"And genius? What is that word?"

"It means intelligent."

His laughter subsided. "You say some strange

things."

"Interesting how our languages are the same, yet… I didn't expect you to speak English."

"English? Is that what you call it?"

I nodded.

"Language has flowed between our worlds for thousands of years," he told me. "Who's to say it wasn't ours first?"

It was a curiosity and didn't matter. What did, was what I was going to do next.

I sat on the log again, and to my surprise, he sat beside me.

"Altrys? What's going on here?"

He didn't say anything for a long time. I allowed him to think, not stirring until he'd made a decision. He'd trust me or he wouldn't. If he did, then I might be able to help and make a good impression on the queen and the people. If not, then I had to find my way back to the capital and start earning trust from there.

I hoped he'd tell me. Whatever was happening out here, helping was just the right thing to do. Dad wouldn't have turned away from someone who needed help, and he definitely wouldn't want me to, either.

"The spirits in the forest," Altrys began. "I've been feeling their presence for days, but you only just noticed them. You are afraid, Elspeth. You're afraid of what you might find in this world and what it will mean for your future."

"Maybe," I told him, "but I'm still here to face it."

Altrys picked up a stick and began stabbing the ground, digging up dirt. "There is a group of extremist Unseelie who are trying to gain a foothold in the Reaches," he said. "Anything and everything that may be suspected activity must be investigated."

"Who are they?"

"They're known as the Chimera."

I tensed, even though I knew I'd hear about them eventually.

"They're fanatical, deadly, and will do anything for power," he went on. "They hide in the shadows, praying to their god of death, claiming they're paving the way for her arrival." He scoffed and shook his head. "It's all nonsense designed to strike fear in the hearts of the people."

I swallowed hard and tightened my fingers into fists. *Praying to their god of death.*

Altrys looked at me, his brow furrowing. "You know of them?"

"I don't have to know them," I told him. "There are people like that in my world, too. They desire power and wealth above all else. They don't care who they ruin to get it, not even if they murder entire races of people."

He tapped a finger on the hilt of my knife. "You've fought people like this before?"

I nodded.

The Fae grunted and I wasn't sure if he was surprised or suspicious. Either way, telling him the truth of who I was wouldn't end well. The god of death had arrived, but not in the way the Chimera had hoped.

"There was a report from the village," Altrys said, nodding towards the signs of civilisation on the other side of the bushes. "I was sent to verify and contain."

"Does it have something to do with the spirits?"

"Perhaps."

"So, is that a yes?"

"You want me to give you a recommendation to the queen in return."

I shrugged. "It wouldn't hurt, but if something is wrong here, then helping without expecting a reward is the right thing to do. Isn't it?"

"Yes." Altrys's silver eyes flashed. "You remain silent. You listen. Observe. Use no magic. If you see something, wait until we are alone to tell me." He pulled the hood of my new cloak over my head and pushed my hair back, hiding it from prying eyes. "And remain as invisible as a shadow, Elspeth from Ireland."

"I can do that," I said, smiling up at him. "No problem."

His sliver eyes narrowed. "I'm putting my trust in you. Don't make me regret it."

"Don't make me regret not letting you take me to the nearest road, and we've got a deal."

Altrys shook his head and turned towards the village. "What have I gotten myself into?"

8

———

Honestly, I'd been expecting more of a fight with Altrys. He'd given in way too quick, but maybe it was a Fae thing.

I wondered if he could see things I couldn't.

We descended the side of the hill and into the valley. Below, the river flowed fast, the creamy blue water full of glacier melt from the mountains above. The Himalayas were one thing, but this range put them to shame.

The village itself was nestled in the lowest part of the valley, beside a large arc in the river. A waterwheel attached to a mill spun in a small canal, a stream of woodsmoke billowed from several stone houses, and sounds of human habitation echoed up the rise.

Curiosity dulled the ache in my bones, and I found I couldn't wait to see what it was like. After all that uncertainty and fear, this world wasn't all that bad, right?

"So, what is your title, exactly?" I asked, following Altrys down the path. "Officer, soldier, investigator, pain in the arse…"

Altrys snorted. "I am a *Shr'lei de Delei'an*. A sword of the queen. The people call us the *Shr'lei*."

"Which word means sword?"

"*Shr'lei.*"

"They call you the swords?"

"Blades." He tapped the eight-pointed star pinned on his cloak. "The sharp point of the queen's justice."

The Fae language was so strange and unfamiliar. I grimaced, thinking how the words were so interchangeable depending on who spoke them. There wasn't a seamless translation into English, either. The closest I'd come to learning another language—besides the Scots Gaelic I cheated at—was French in year seven and eight at school. I could still count to ten, but Altrys wasn't interested in French numbers.

"*Shr*…" I stumbled over the odd grouping of sounds. "*Shr'lei.*"

Altrys snorted. "You'll get there."

We crossed a stone bridge that arched over the river, merging with a wide road.

Ahead, the village emerged from the iridescent greenery. First were small farms and stables, then the grey stone buildings of the village centre, most of which rose two to three stories high. Wooden beams and trusses held up windows and doorframes, ferns and other vines grew from cracks in the masonry, and the street was partially paved with cobblestones and a thick layer of mud.

A man with long, brown hair walked past with a large, black, wolf-like dog with silver fur along its spine. Children streaked across our path, chasing a golden bird that looked a lot like a metallic chicken. A woman with pink hair lingered in a window, watching us walk by with an air of guarded curiosity.

The village was alive with earthy tones, but the people I saw were nothing like me, apart from the one woman with pink hair. They were all like Altrys— brown to black hair and an echo of power that seemed beyond their grasp.

My boots squelched in the mud of the well-worn road, my gaze flickering here and there, unable to focus on any one thing. Light posts reminiscent of Victorian era gas lamps. Familiar animals with strange colouring. A reverence to the wild nature of the place they'd built the village. Fae dressed in simple, yet elegant garb. A guard troop dressed in shining silver armour. A young woman selling posies of wildflowers outside a bakery.

I'd stepped into a Medieval fantasy world.

I stopped in my tracks as a man rode by on a chestnut horse. The horse's hair was so dense, it looked like it was covered in moss, and its mane flowed in silken waves.

"Stop staring," Altrys hissed.

"But… they look like they've been Photoshopped."

"And stop talking so strangely," he added, wrenching me away. "It's just a horse."

"And that chicken was gold," I went on. "Next you'll be telling me they lay golden eggs."

He blinked. "And what colour do they lay them in your world?"

My mouth fell open. "Are you serious?"

"Focus, Elspeth," Altrys said, pulling me underneath the eave of an alley between buildings. "I'm here on summons by the queen. If you want to help, then use your eyes and ears for more than contemplating the colour of chickens."

"I can't help it. This place is strange, yet somehow, familiar."

"It's your blood that remembers," he told me. "See that building at the end of the street?"

I followed his nod towards a fancy stone façade at the far end of the thoroughfare. Banners hung down either side of the double doors—elongated pennants in emerald bordered in earthy brown, with an unknown motif in the centre.

"That is the residence of the Lor'andann of Un Alari."

"The mayor? You want me to stand with you while you speak to the mayor of fantasy land?" My heart skipped a beat and Altrys pushed my shoulder, wrenching my attention back to him.

"Speak like that and I'll leave you outside with the horses and put a shovel in your hands."

I swallowed hard. "Un Alari. Is that the name of this place?"

He nodded. "The Lor'andann governs this place and the lands surrounding in the name of the queen. I must officially present myself and question his household."

"You can do that? Just walk in and demand your questions be answered?"

"Within reason."

I took a deep breath. "What do you want me to do?"

"Watch. Listen. You have magic, Elspeth. If you truly want to help, then use it to measure the truth in their answers. See what cannot be seen. Hear what cannot be spoken. There is more to being a *shr'lei* than unsheathing a sword."

"But you will if you have to."

"Only as a last resort."

I nodded. If the Chimera were here, meddling in the affairs of Un Alari, then a fight was what it may come to. And I hoped that it didn't.

Altrys led me down the street, walking tall. He paid no attention to the stares he received from the villagers, confident in his status. When we reached the doors of the Lor'andann's residence, he slammed his fist on the doors three times. *Boom, boom, boom.*

I kept my hood up as the doors swung open, my hands shaking at the thought of what we might find inside, and we stepped across the threshold into a grand hall.

Immediately, I saw the male Fae, such was his presence. He sat in a high-backed chair on an elevated platform at the end of the room. The seat had the look of a throne—the top of it towered above him, the point carved with the same symbol on the banners outside, which I now saw *was* a stag.

The man stared at us as we began to walk the length of the hall, his silver eyes piercing even from this distance. His waist-length hair shone like ice, each strand so white it took on whatever colour reflected in the air—now it was backed with the mahogany of the throne, his tresses glowing with menacing fire.

Long fingers stretched over the arms of the chair, and his breast shone with silver scales—an armoured tunic. He also wore a crown made of twisted wood, with carved points resembling deer antlers, imbedded with silver and jewels.

I gathered this was the Lor'andann of Un Alari, but he'd styled himself as a king of the woodlands. As we approached, I wondered how kosher that was with the queen. Maybe not as much as he had hoped, considering he wore armour to receive Altrys, a *Shr'lei de Delei'an*.

Managing to prise my gaze away from the Lor'andann, I counted the members of the guard who stood on either side of the hall, positioned between the beams holding the vaulted ceiling in place. Six.

A balcony ran the entire way around the room, emerald and brown banners hanging in regular intervals from the balustrade. Wreaths and garlands hung everywhere, the woven leaves and branches dotted with white flowers resembling lilies and tiny pinprick blooms that reminded me of baby's breath.

But it was the light that made the hall magical. Tiny orbs floated overhead, bobbing up and down amongst the eaves, casting a clear white glow over the warm wood finishes below.

It was stunning, but my senses began to stir as a woman stepped up onto the platform and stood beside the Lor'andann.

She was darker in colouring—her hair was such a deep red that it almost looked black. Her tresses had been twisted into elaborate braids and pinned with shimmering jewels, and a tight silver choker in the same design as the crown on the Lor'andann's head adorned her long neck. Her dress matched his armour, silver scales sewn onto a long-sleeved ebony gown. This must be his wife.

Walking the length of the hall seemed to take an age, and we finally stopped before the foot of the platform. I stood a step behind Altrys and kept my head down, but my eyes and ears remained sharp.

Altrys bowed, and I hastily followed.

"Altrys, *Shr'lei de Delei'an*," the Lor'andann said, his voice silky. "Welcome to Un Alari—the village of the Silver Mountains. It was about time you made your presence known to me. You've been lingering in my forest for three days."

"Forgive me, Lor'andann," Altrys replied. "I had

a long journey and wished to pay my respects to the elements."

This seemed to please him some. "And who is it that you have brought with you?" I tensed as his gaze moved to me.

"This is my *shride*. Elspeth, *Shride de Shr'lei*."

I bowed again but said nothing, my hood still firmly covering my hair. Now that I was closer, his presence had the overbearing weight any person of authority held. He was arrogant, confident, and cold. Perfectly put together, apart from a stain on the collar of his armoured jerkin, the Lor'andann was a picture of regal power.

He pursed his lips at my silence and gestured to the woman beside him. "May I present Larel, my wife."

The woman inclined her head slightly. "Enchanted, *Shr'lei*." Like the Lor'andann, her voice was musical, though soft.

The Lor'andann waved his hand to silence her. "And what brings you to my realm, *Shr'lei*?"

"Queen Niarisshia sent me in regards to reports of unrest in the region," Altrys explained.

"Unrest?" His eyes flashed. "There is no unrest here."

"Three days in the forest would suggest otherwise. The spirits are restless."

"The spirits of the forest are our guardians," Larel said. "They are welcome here."

"The spirits of the forest speak to me and only

me," the Lor'andann stated, shooting a fierce glare at his wife. "I hear their wisdom and impart it upon the people. They are grateful to hear the words of the elementals."

"I don't disagree," Altrys said. "Though it would be wise to take caution, Lor'andann."

My gaze moved to Larel, who'd laid a hand on her husband's shoulder. Her lips twitched and her silver eyes shifted to mine. "And what does your *shride* say, Altrys?"

Altrys opened his mouth, but the Lor'andann held up his hand. "I would hear her words, *Shr'lei*. Let her speak."

Oh, shite. What would Rory say? Better yet, what would Delilah say? I thought back to my lessons in the library with my grandmother, my mind working like lightning.

"To be cautious is wise," I told them, "for it allows us to see what cannot be seen in haste."

The Lor'andann smiled faintly, though Larel's gaze became colder than the glaciers on the mountains above Un Alari.

"There is no unrest here," he declared, his voice echoing throughout the hall. "Your journey has been in haste, Altrys, *Shr'lei de Delei'an*. I'm afraid you will have to return to Queen Niarisshia without a trophy to hang from the tip of your blade."

"Once a *shr'lei* has been dispatched, they must complete their task thoroughly," Altrys said. "I intend to honour my oath, Lor'andann, regardless."

"Then go," he said. "Fulfil your oath, Altrys, *Shr'lei de Delei'an*, but know that I will not suffer the peace of the forest."

"*A'ladrei*, Lor'andann," he replied. Altrys bowed low and I hastened to follow suit.

He strode away from the dais and I had to lengthen my stride to match his speed. It seemed the exit was just as important as the entrance.

The doors closed behind us with a boom, letting me know exactly what the Lor'andann thought of us.

"Did I say the wrong thing?" I asked as we walked down the street.

"Yes and no. What you said was wise, but not what he wanted to hear."

I sighed. It was too late to worry about it now. "He was wearing armour. And what was with the crown? Is it just me, or was that a step too far?"

"I think he may be cursed," Altrys said, ignoring my question. Or then again, it may have been an answer.

"Cursed?" I asked. "Curses are a thing?"

"Most certainly."

"Well, where I come from, they aren't. At least, I've always thought they were just things people made up to scare others." Maybe the Witches knew about them because the Druids certainly didn't have any equivalent. "How can you even tell?"

"Everything about that meeting was wrong."

I raised my eyebrows. "So, let's just say he's cursed. How does it work exactly?"

"A curse is magical intent designed to cause harm, suffering, or control," Altrys explained. "There's a thousand different ways to conjure one and to bind it to the victim."

"So to prove it, we're looking for a needle in a haystack."

The Fae narrowed his eyes at me.

"A little thing in an ocean of big things." I spread my arms wide.

"I understand," he told me.

"Okay, so…"

Altrys looked towards the forest. "The spirits are connected in some way. They're influencing him somehow."

"What's that got to do with a curse?" I asked.

"He believes he's speaking with nature and the spirits are a conduit between him and the elements. The spirits are restless and shouldn't be there."

"They should be at rest?"

He nodded. "And he seems determined to let them roam, no matter the harm they could cause the people in his charge."

"Harm?"

"Possession, mutilation, death."

I snorted. All the finest things about being haunted by Fae elemental ghosts, then.

"Did you notice the blood on his collar?" I asked. "The fabric was dark, but there was a stain."

Altrys nodded. "That it was there at all is sloppy."

"What does it mean?"

He glanced at me. "Blood sacrifice."

My eyes widened.

"It must be well advanced if he didn't bother to check his clothing before speaking to us," Altrys went on. "It's an ancient practice, but a powerful one. Fae have been known to become so lost to it, they become twisted beyond recognition. That was why it became forbidden by law."

"Well, his wife seems to be all for it," I mused. "Do you think she has something to do with it?"

"Perhaps. People here are pious. The forest is sacred, and any sign is taken literally. She could just believe the same way the Lor'andann does, just without the influence of a curse."

"Another form of extremist religion?"

"I wouldn't say extremist, but they will defend their beliefs if they have to. This is tied closely to them."

"So tread carefully." I sighed, remembering the things Skye told me about the trickery of Fae. Whatever was going on here was masterfully crafted. It may be a curse making the Lor'andann do things he normally wouldn't, or it may be his deliberate attempt to wrest more power from the queen and spark an uprising... or it may be a Chimera plot.

Thinking back to the way he spoke, I would have believed the guy no questions asked. That was my naivety speaking, though. Altrys was convinced and he was a *shr'lei,* who hopefully came with a swathe of experience. If he said something wasn't right, then something wasn't right.

I was totally out of my depth, but I was determined to try. I had the power of death at my fingertips, not only as the black sun but as a Druid… but would Altrys understand? My father was ruthlessly hunted for his Colour. Who was to say Altrys wouldn't covet it as well?

"What now?" I asked, watching the comings and goings of the village.

"We walk amongst the people and hear their stories," Altrys replied. "We'll go back to the forest at nightfall. I would like to investigate those spirits further."

I checked my hood and made sure my hair was still hidden. A part of me was excited to see more of the village and learn about the people here, but the other bit was worried.

"You said you intended to honour your oath," I murmured. "The Lor'andann seemed angry about it. Why?"

"He doesn't have the power to stop me from investigating," Altrys told me. "Not openly."

I grimaced and looked over my shoulder. "Do you expect trouble?"

"Yes," the Fae replied, "most certainly."

9

————

Altrys and I spent the rest of the day wandering around Un Alari.

To my confusion, Altrys didn't speak to anyone. He just watched and listened, going from store to store, purchasing me strange Fae pastries from the bakery, paying the seamstress a visit to thank her for the clothing he'd bought for me, complimenting a man on his horses, and generally, making a show of lazing about.

Not once did he question anyone openly about the Lor'andann or the spirits in the forest.

He must have a reason for it, but I couldn't see the point. We weren't going to learn anything by staying silent.

Instead, I turned my attention to the village, trying to work out how things operated.

The bulk of the people here seemed to be De'ashlide. To my foreigner's eyes, they appeared similar to regular humans, though their features seemed more angular and there was an overwhelming attractiveness ratio. On the surface, life and the people in it were idyllic.

Under the beautiful exterior, another story brewed. It was just as Altrys said. There was a divide between the Shri'danann and the De'ashlide, though very few of the former appeared to call Un Alari home.

I saw a woman with yellow tresses, a man with short, cropped crimson hair, and a little girl with magenta braids. I sensed an air of quiet apprehension around them, and for good reason—they were outnumbered and magic wouldn't save them if the entire village decided they wanted the Shri'danann to leave.

The little girl was handing out little sprigs of carefully arranged leaves and flowers. When she saw us wandering past, she ran up to Altrys and stuffed one into his hands.

"*A'ladrei,*" he told her, resting a hand on her head.

She looked at me and her cheeks heated. I smiled at her, but it only caused her to let out a squawk and run away like a bolt of lightning had struck her feet.

"What did I do?" I asked, feeling like I'd been punched in the gut. I really took things a little too much to heart.

"You're a woman *Shride de Shr'lei,*" Altrys said with a chuckle. He handed me the flowers.

I snorted. "I see the gender divide is alive and well in your world, too."

The *shr'lei* rolled his eyes and led me across the square to the village tavern. It looked like a traditional English pub mixed with something out of a fantasy novel. Vines laden with green leaves and red berries wound around the wooden beams holding up the crooked verandah. The vines snaked their way onto the roof and over the second and third stories to the very top of the building.

"Keep your hood up," Altrys said.

I waved a hand over my face. "I'm a shadow. Are we going to get drunk?"

"No."

He pushed open the door and led me inside. Chatter lulled as we moved through the mess of tables and chairs, a hundred pairs of silver eyes following our footsteps.

We sat at a table in the back, and a waitress set down two mugs in front of us before moving off.

Picking up the mug, I sniffed at the brown liquid inside. It was sweet and fruity, not at all like the barley and hops I was expecting.

"What is it?" I asked Altrys.

"*Aru'de*," he replied. "Wine."

Well, you may be the master of death, but you only live once, Elspeth. I sipped at the liquid, the sugary fruit rolling over my taste buds, which exploded like a nuclear bomb.

"*Bloody hell*," I hissed and wiped my tongue on the back of my sleeve. "It's like drinking syrup."

"Careful," Altrys warned. "It's potent to the unwary."

"Potent is the right word."

"Altrys, *Shr'lei de Delei'an*."

I looked up to find an unknown Fae standing opposite with her hands on her hips. It was the woman with pink hair who I'd seen that morning.

She was small and delicate, with perfect skin and sharp silver eyes. Her hair was the kind of pink that went with fairy floss at a carnival, but her expression definitely didn't. The clothes she wore weren't exactly the girly type, either. Her tight grey trousers, black and silver corset, and black silk choker would have her marked as either a dominatrix or a goth off to a night club, but in this world, it seemed she worked at the tavern. When I looked around at the other staff, I noted that they all wore similar outfits.

Where in the world was I? A tavern or a cabaret?

"Well," the woman said, sitting across from us. "I heard you were lingering. It's nice to see you finally showing your handsome face."

"Adrielle." He nodded sharply.

The woman sighed and rolled her eyes. "Are you still angry with me? It's been a long time since——"

Altrys coughed loudly and nodded towards me.

"Hi," I said, lifting my hand in a wave.

"Adrielle, this is Elspeth. She's my *Shride de Shr'lei*." Suddenly, he sounded tired.

Her glance flickered to my hood, then back to my face.

"I'm new," I told her. "He wants me to be a shadow." Altrys grunted and I grimaced. "A silent shadow."

"I guess you're here for the spirits, then," she said with a sigh.

"And?" he prodded.

"And I likely know just as much as you do."

"It was you who sent the report," he whispered.

She nodded. "Something has changed here. A seed has been planted. The air is cold and the earth is dry. It will begin here if you don't stop it, Altrys."

He lowered his gaze and picked up his mug. They said nothing more about it, but I sensed their actions towards one another told a deeper story.

Adrielle rose, her expression closing. "If that is all, *shr'lei*," she said loudly, "then I bid you a good evening."

Altrys said nothing as she walked away. He said even less to me.

I watched as Adrielle moved around openly, not afraid of the De'ashlide who made up the bulk of the villagers. They weren't hostile to her like they'd been me, but maybe it was because she lived here and had earned their trust. Everyone loved a bartender.

"*Slàinte*," I muttered, raising my cup.

I sipped at the wine, finally developing a liking for it… or maybe it was because my taste buds had malfunctioned.

"Don't drink all of that," Altrys warned. "We're leaving soon."

"We're not allowed to be drunk on the job?"

"I wasn't being heavy handed when I said that stuff is potent."

"You say that like you've had your own experience." He smirked and I let out a laugh. "Altrys, you party animal, you!"

"We need our senses to remain sharp, Elspeth. There's no telling what we may find in the dark."

I shivered and set down the mug. When he said it like that, it felt like I'd just become a character in a horror movie. We'd go out into the woods and get hacked to pieces by an axe murderer. I wondered if the Fae had a word for that.

I glanced across the room at Adrielle, my senses tingling. What had I gotten myself into?

"*A'ladrei*… what does that mean?"

"Hmm?"

"*A'ladrei*. You said it to the little girl outside."

Altrys looked in Adrielle's direction. "Thank you," he said. "It means thank you."

<hr>

When the sun finally went down and darkness fell over Un Alari, Altrys and I went back to the forest.

We slunk out of the village, keeping to the shadows in case anyone was watching, and then we ventured into the depths of the wilderness, leaving behind well-worn paths.

I hoped Altrys knew where he was going because I had no idea how we were going to find our way back in the pitch-black.

"Adrielle seems nice," I mused as I followed his careful steps in the dark.

"She's a good person."

She's a good person? I sighed. Men were as dumb here as they were back on Earth.

"She already knew you were in the village," I said. "I saw her looking at us when we arrived this morning. She was playing it cool."

Altrys said nothing, but I noticed that his shoulders tensed. There was history there and a lot of it.

"What did Adrielle do to you?" I asked.

"She took her own path a long time ago."

"She thought you were in Un Alari for her, you know. Was she your girlfriend?"

He scowled, confused. "Girlfriend?"

"You don't say that? What do you call it here, then?"

"Call what?" he demanded.

"The person you love."

Altrys expression darkened, warning me that I was on unstable ground.

"Adrielle has the gift of foresight," he said instead. "She believes Un Alari is where the war will begin."

A chill ran through my body. "War? What war?"

"The last war between the Shri'danann and the Chimera legions."

"What about the De'ashlide?"

"They are not included," he replied.

I snorted. "You think they can't fight just because they have no magic?"

"It's dangerous to stand against magic. If they were recruited, they would die in vast numbers. Despite their hate for us, we will protect them."

I found it curious that he regarded himself amongst the Shri'danann, though he'd said he had little magic being half like me. Maybe it was another quirk about this world I didn't understand yet.

"Adrielle has lived in the Reaches for a long time," Altrys went on. "She knows the land and the players better than most. If she says something isn't right, then we would do best to listen."

I stepped over a fallen log. "Fair enough."

We ventured into the dense forest for another ten minutes or so before I began to feel cool fingers brush against my powers. The veil stirred, causing the blackness below the surface of my Colour to ripple. The sensation was so clear, my heart sped up. I now understood that it would be harder to keep the black sun down here.

I grasped Altrys's arm. "They're ahead."

"You can sense them?"

I nodded. "You were right about this world. I'm more… sensitive here."

Ahead, the darkness began to ebb with cool blue

light that only grew as we approached. I wasn't expecting the spirits to have form, but now that I saw it, I began to see why Altrys was so concerned.

We crouched in the undergrowth, watching the lights dance through the woods. First there were two, then three, then a fourth orb joined, twisting and racing around the others.

They were beautiful to watch, but I knew as well as any that beautiful things could be just as evil as the ugly. It was the core of a thing that mattered. The surface was just a layer, like the cloak around my shoulders.

They didn't feel like dead things, but I wasn't sure how to tell Altrys without implicating myself. But there was a chance they weren't supposed to feel like death.

It seemed like the Fae believed spirits lingered because they wanted to guide and protect the people, but the forest seemed off. Like this place had a precise order to it and one piece was slightly skewed. Perhaps that was the difference between a spiritual connection and a haunting.

Hauntings tended to be problematic and sometimes violent. Poltergeists, demonic entities, and other evil spirits came to mind, thanks to all those ghost hunting television shows I used to binge back home. I wasn't going to get any EMF or electronic voice phenomena here, but I had the next best thing —the veil.

I glanced at Altrys, wondering how much I could

get away with before he caught on that I wasn't telling him the whole story. He was sharp, so I guessed very little.

"The Lor'andann thinks the spirits live here peacefully," I said. "But they're haunting this place, aren't they?"

Altrys nodded. "And they're not elemental."

"Then they're Fae souls?"

"Possibly."

It would explain the odd feeling I felt, but I'd seen the souls of the Chimera. They were Fae and technically, they should all be the same on a fundamental level.

"What if they aren't sprits?" I asked, hoping for some clarity on the situation.

Altrys glanced at me. "What makes you think they aren't?"

I shrugged. "Just a suggestion."

"They can't be anything else," he said after a moment. "There are ancient things… but they're creatures long gone from this world."

"Ancient things?" I lingered beside him, my skin prickling at the thought.

He shook his head. "A story for another time."

Now I was beginning to doubt how much Altrys knew about what he was getting us into.

"So they're the souls of lost Fae, bound to this place by a curse to trick the Lor'andann."

"It seems to be so."

"But why?"

"To drive him mad and weaken his hold over Un Alari. An unstable ruler is an opportunity."

I swallowed hard. *An opportunity for the Chimera to swoop in and take control.*

"The people would never support an outright coup," he added. "They wouldn't notice a gradual takeover; they would support it."

The orbs blinked out and the forest fell into darkness a split-second before something large collided with Altrys. I didn't have time to react as he hurtled across the clearing and rolled to a stop.

Metal scraped against metal behind me and I wrenched my knife free as I rose to my feet.

Four masked men slunk from the shadows, their black clothing concealing their movements. Their swords were the only thing that reflected the sliver of light from the moon above, but I had my senses to guide me. If I focused… I hoped it would be enough.

Right then, I wished I knew some swear words in Fae. It was the first thing anyone learned in a new language, right?

Altrys groaned as he stood and pulled the sword from the scabbard on his back.

"You should have returned to the capital, *shr'lei*," one of the men murmured. "You were warned."

"Who sent you?" Altrys asked. "The Lor'andann? Or was it Larel?"

None of the men replied. They circled us with an unmistakable intent. We'd poked our noses where they weren't wanted and now, we were going to die.

Adrielle was right. It was going to begin here.

I had one ace up my sleeve, though I hoped I didn't have to play it yet. If these were Chimera agents, then they had just made a big mistake.

They attacked all at once, putting my meagre skills to the ultimate test. Twin swords seemingly came at me from all directions and it was all I could do to duck and weave, let alone find an opening to strike.

Altrys slammed his blade through a Fae's gut, a pained cry tearing through the air. I faltered as I felt the attacker's soul tear from his body and pass into the next world. *That was new.*

A blade streaked through the air and I ducked the savage blow, the metal singing as the Fae tried to take my head off my shoulders.

I nearly stumbled—but kept pushing—as another soul was torn from the body of a Fae Altrys was fighting.

One of the Fae I was fighting peeled away and went for Altrys. The split-second where I wasn't being worn down by two swords gave me the opening I was looking for.

My knife plunged into the thigh of my opponent, the edge of the blade sawing past bone. Jerking it free, I flipped the hilt in my hand and struck, this time slicing between ribs and into my attacker's heart.

I gasped as his soul departed and pushed him away. The body fell to the forest floor with a thud.

A crash across the clearing turned my head as Altrys fell hard. A dark shadow loomed over him, and

I snatched up the discarded sword at my feet, swapping my knife to my less dominant hand.

The masked Fae lifted his arms, holding his blade high and I broke out into a run. It flew towards Altrys's neck and I knew he didn't have time to move out of the way. *He was about to die.*

Grasping for the veil, I threw up my hand and the familiar chill of death spread through my fingers and up my arm. My boots skidded in the soft earth and I froze, my heart swelling with the pure power that rushed through me.

The Fae gasped and dropped his sword, caught in my web even though I wasn't touching him.

"Altrys, *move*," I commanded, my voice rasping with the currents of death.

He scrambled backward, his heels digging into the mud. His eyes widened as he glanced between me and the man. "What—"

The veil rose from the forest floor, bubbling like tar, and began to greedily twist around the Fae's ankles.

I like it here. I like it here. I like it here.

"*Shut up*," I hissed at the voices.

"*Elspeth.*"

I ignored Altrys's panicked warning.

"You dare attack a *Shr'lei de Delei'an*?" I rasped, stepping towards the masked Fae. "You dare attack *me*?"

I tore off his bandana and wasn't surprised when I saw familiar grey skin and pointed teeth. The twisted face of a Chimera stared back at me and I looked into his silver irises with my own blackened eyes.

"*Liash li Ashli*," the Chimera cried.

"See me. *I am here*."

"*Liash——*"

I closed my fingers, curling them into a tight fist. The man gasped, his mouth gaping as I tore his soul from his body and pushed it across the veil.

Cracks shattered across his face, tearing his skin as his mortal body turned to ash. His cheeks caved in and his skull crumbled; then, as the veil receded, the rest of his body dissolved into ash.

I stood over Altrys, my chest heaving. He stared up at me, his expression unreadable.

The jig was up. I'd exposed myself as the Big Bad Wolf. The Chimera's god of death had arrived, and the war to end all wars would either begin or end in Un Alari.

Altrys had two choices—he would either kill me or let me go.

Finally, I held out my hand…

And he took it.

10

A ltrys buried the bodies where they lay.

They had no identification or talismans—just their swords and cotton masks—so there was nothing else to be done.

I stood silently, watching as he revealed his power to me for the first time. His weakened Shri'danann legacy called on the elements of the forest, opening up the earth, coaxing the roots and worms to rise and consume the Fae who'd attacked us.

The ash of the Fae I'd destroyed with the black sun dissolved, bracken growing over it all.

Finally, he rose and began walking through the woods, leaving the now quiet spirits and the battle behind us.

I had no other option but to follow.

By the time Altrys stopped, we were deep into the wilderness. No one would find us in the dense twists and turns of the ancient landscape. Un Alari was a distant speck nestled in a valley at least a two-hours' walk away.

No one had ever set foot here.

"*Liash li Ashli,*" he murmured, unable to meet my gaze. "I know exactly who you are."

"No, you don't," I said. "You know *what* I am. You know nothing of *who* I am or *why* I am."

"I do know you called on death to kill that Chimera."

I shoved him hard enough to make him stumble. "What I did was save your life, despite the fact you might turn around and kill me anyway."

"You were waiting for me in the forest yesterday," Altrys said. "That whole scene—"

"I was not!" I cried. "I never lied about anything!"

"You lied by omission, Elspeth."

"*For good reason.*"

His eyes flashed in the moonlight. "Give me one good reason why I should trust you."

"I had no reason to trust you, but here we are a day later, and I'm risking everything to save your life. A thank you wouldn't go astray!"

His expression darkened and he took an aggressive step towards me. "You are the *Liash li Ashli.* You're here to help them take over our world."

I hissed at him and took a step forwards. I wouldn't let anyone intimidate me. I wouldn't let anyone put words into my mouth. *I wouldn't let anyone paint me into a prophesied corner.*

"I'm not here to help the Chimera," I told him.

"I'm here to stop them, just like I did in my own world. I won't be their pawn, *or your queen's*. Don't even get me started on that pompous arse, the Lor'andann. Give that man a mirror and he'd get lost looking at himself."

He said nothing. He didn't even twitch.

"They've hunted me my whole life, Altrys. They murdered my father. They waged war against my people. *My family…* the people who gave me a home after I lost everything… The Chimera murdered so many of them because they wanted me. I would *never* help them."

The hood of my cloak had fallen off during the fight and I picked up a strand of emerald green hair. I thought of all the people I'd seen today, the Shri'danann Seelie of Un Alari. Yellow, crimson, and magenta. Adrielle's pink tresses. The warmth…

I held up my hands and the phantom chill of the veil made them tremble.

"I'm Unseelie, aren't I?" I murmured.

Altrys looked away. It was all the answer I needed.

"It's my hair that marks me, not just my power. That's why people were treating Adrielle like a friend. She's Seelie."

I couldn't believe that I could be predisposed to evil just because I was born a Dark Fae. The world wasn't black and white; there were shades of grey. No one was perfectly good or perfectly evil. Everyone was the hero of their own story.

"Why did you help me?" Altrys's voice was quiet,

his deep tone hardly audible over the serene rustling of the forest's night sounds.

"Because you helped me, no questions asked," I replied. "Because I wanted to help. Because my father taught me…" Tears sprang into my eyes unbidden. "'*I have the power to help*,' he said to me. '*And when the Earth and her creatures cry out in pain, we should answer with our whole hearts.*'"

Altrys was silent yet again and I felt the urge to slap some sense into him, to make him see that I was on his side. I wasn't some evil god of death. I was simply Elspeth Odhweine, trying her best to stop a mass genocide.

"Why did *you* help *me*?" I asked, turning his question back on him. "If you really believe I'm an evil Unseelie, then why bother?"

"My oath demands it."

"Is that all?" I'd only known him a day, yet it felt as if he'd plunged a knife into my heart.

I tightened my hands into fists. Why was that?

Because you like him.

"Yes."

I snorted. Fae didn't like to lie. It sullied their honour.

"What does your precious oath demand now?" I taunted.

"We'll make camp here," he said, ignoring me.

I had no idea how to build a fire, so I sat in the shadows fighting back tears of frustration as Altrys gathered fallen wood and sticks. He built a well-practiced teepee of sorts within a circle of stones, then struck a spark into some kindling at the base. Soon, a small fire was crackling.

He sat on the opposite side of the flames and turned his gaze onto me. "Tell me your story, Elspeth from Ireland. The *real* story."

"Odhweine," I said, wrapping my cloak around my body as if it were a shield. "My name is Elspeth Odhweine and I'm not from Ireland."

"The first lie you allowed me to believe."

"Everything else I told you is true. I never lied about anything. You were the one who decided I was from Ireland. The bits I left out…"

Altrys waited.

"I didn't grow up around other Fae," I told him. "I never knew what I was until…" I counted in my head. I arrived in Scotland in January and it was late July when we left Earth. "Seven months or so ago."

"The hair didn't give it away?"

"No. My hair used to be auburn. I used to be ordinary. A… my world's version of a De'ashlide. I think… I think all magic there came from other worlds. Magic is secret."

I shivered, wishing I could sink into a hole in the earth and never come out. I had to tell Altrys the truth. All of it. The Druids, the Chimera, my father's portals, my mother. If I wanted his trust, then I couldn't hold back.

And it frightened me more than facing Mindel and the Chimera in that cave had.

The Druids. Rory. Ignis. They'd come here for me and now everything was messed up.

I felt bad about not thinking about them. They must be in the capital fretting over where I was. Ignis wouldn't be able to find me, just like I wasn't able to phase. I wondered if Elmarrin even cared. He would have reported to Queen Niarisshia by now. What would she say?

Looking up at Altrys, I swallowed hard. "Can I trust you?"

"I didn't kill you. Isn't that a good enough indicator?"

I guessed it was.

"I'm only half Fae," I told him.

He raised his eyebrows. "And what's the other half?"

"Druid. My father was a Druid."

Altrys's brow furrowed in confusion.

I pushed my hand out from underneath my cloak and held it out, palm up. Calling on my Colours, a thread of holographic blue and purple light began to pool, then a thread rose, following the guidance of my intent.

"The Druids are a peaceful people," I murmured as the prism grew. "They honour the wisdom of nature. They tend to the earth and help it grow. They're travellers. Nomads who walk the paths between worlds, seeking knowledge and understanding. Spirit."

Altrys watched the spirals and lines grow in the palm of my hand, his expression shocked.

"My people were separated on the journey to their homeland," I continued. "Lost, they were forced to find a new home in an alternate world and remain adrift, hoping that one day they would find the way back. Through that search, my father stumbled upon your world. He found the Fae and fell in love with my mother. The love between them ignited the Chimera's desire to hunt the Druids… and me. It was all he could do to escape and go into hiding. He never told me. He… He died for me, but I never knew why. Not until I met the Druids."

Dad. The rose shimmered, the red bud unfurling into a full bloom.

"There's more to me than commanding death," I murmured. "As a Druid, I have the ability to shape space and time. This flower is made of Colour… our word for magic. This Colour is the very fabric of reality."

"You can… *You can open portals.*"

I closed my hand around the flower, absorbing the prism. "To your queen and the Chimera, I am the only weapon that matters, but I'm more than that. I am more than a prophecy. A prophecy I renounced the moment I chose to destroy the Chimera on Earth. I choose not to become a pawn in a war that can only end in genocide. I won't allow it."

"Then why did you come here?" Altrys asked.

"Niarisshia would have known who you were the moment you stood before her."

"Maybe. Maybe not." I snorted. "I didn't lie about that, you know. I came here to learn about being a Fae. To find my mother. To make sense of this thing I've become." I stared into the fire, watching the flames flicker in the breeze. "I came to stop the Chimera. Death is just the next life, but everyone has the right to live in this one. Nature is the only thing that should take souls across the veil. You saw what I became… I don't want to be this."

Altrys's anger had seemed to have dissolved by now but had ignited a curiosity I wasn't sure how to take.

"The prophecy…" he began. "I've heard what the Chimera worship, but not the words. What is it?"

"*Born of ashes, dead in darkness, a soul who bridges the gap has the power to destroy Druid and Fae alike. When the black sun rises, death will choose the hand of fate.*"

"The black sun," he murmured. "Adrielle was right. Perhaps—"

"Foresight isn't prophecy," I told him. "Foresight can be changed. If she believes the Chimera's war will begin here, then I will stop it, with or without you."

The fire popped, sending sparks into the air.

Taking a deep breath, I calmed myself, soothing my heartbeat back to a normal rhythm.

"I can feel them die," I murmured, shivering. "I…"

Altrys shifted. "You haven't before?"

I shook my head. "It's this place… This world…"

"I've heard stories that Fae power is weaker on the other side. You must be careful."

"I know. Walking in death isn't as peaceful as it sounds. The currents can sweep you away if you're not careful."

He tensed but didn't press. I'd revealed more than enough for one evening.

"Your power…" I didn't know how to ask him.

"My mother had an affinity for growing things," he said, sensing I wanted to know his story; after all, I'd told him mine. "She was sent to a temple as a girl and learned the ways of the elementals. When she met my father, she was a priestess."

"Was it forbidden?"

Altrys nodded. "In more ways than one would expect. He was De'ashlide."

"What happened to them?"

"My mother was sent away to have her child—me—in secret. My father… he was run off and forbidden to see her again."

My heart swelled. "I'm sorry."

"When I was five years old, I was sent to the capital to train as a *Shr'lei de Delei'an*. That has been my life ever since."

"Five years old?" My mouth fell open. "But you were only a child."

"It is our way." He didn't seem put out by it, like it was just another difference between worlds.

"Do you see your mother?"

He shook his head. "And I'm afraid I don't know anything about yours. If I knew, I would tell you."

"You believe me?"

He looked at me, the firelight playing a strange shadow across his features. "You're not lying."

"And you're avoiding the question."

His lips quirked. "You're too clever for me, Elspeth Odhweine."

I waited, my shoulders heavy.

"I don't want to believe this is truth," he said after a moment. "Because if it is, then the battle that looms on the horizon will touch all things. This world will suffer and it has already suffered a great deal."

I remembered Slye telling me about the civil war between the Seelie and Unseelie, and the unification and reformation under the previous queen, Aibell. The specifics were lost on me, but I had a vivid imagination. The rise of the Chimera had already caused enough chaos and now my arrival heralded another wave.

"Believe me," I drawled, "I don't want to harm anyone."

"Then our mission here is of the highest priority."

I looked up, my eyes widening. "Our mission?"

He nodded. "There must be a reason the portal transported you here. Adrielle's visions are rarely false. It's all connected."

"You and Adrielle…" My cheeks heated and I nestled into my cloak, trying to hide the flush from Altrys.

"Adrielle and I were lovers," he said, staring into the fire. "You were right about that, but I was a little too De'ashlide for her family for it to last."

"It shouldn't matter." I felt a stab of anger on his behalf. It seemed as if history had almost repeated.

"It does matter."

"*It shouldn't.*"

"It was a long time ago, Elspeth. We have changed. Our paths have crossed now, but what we had is all but a memory. We couldn't overcome the obstacles sent to test us. Our future wasn't destined, and we have both made peace with it."

It still wasn't fair.

"And now?" I asked.

His eyes shone brilliant silver in the half-light. "And now, Elspeth Odhweine, we are even."

11

The forest was silent in the wake of the violence and heartache we'd bared upon it.

Neither I nor Altrys seemed able to sleep, so we sat by the campfire well into the night, listening to the sounds of the wilderness around us. I allowed my senses to ebb out into the air, paranoid more masked Fae would leap out of the shadows…but no one came. Nothing stirred and the spirits we'd seen lingered someplace far away.

We were alone.

"Altrys?"

His head rose.

"Where did you get the scar on your jaw?"

He smirked and rubbed a thumb over the chip in his flesh. "A fight. Where else?"

I snorted. Taking my knife out of its scabbard, I inspected the edge. Anything to take my mind off the attack and calm my nerves.

Altrys watched me closely. "What are the markings on your blade?"

Handing him the knife hilt-first, I replied, "Runes."

His brow creased and he traced the lines and angles with his fingertip. "What do they mean?"

"It's a prayer to the Druid homeland, *Thríbhís Mhór*. It honours the earth, sea, and sky which binds it all together."

"Are the symbols a part of your language?"

I nodded.

He studied the runes for a long time, as if he were committing them to memory. Perhaps he was paying homage.

"It belonged to my…" I hesitated. What did I call Rory? He wasn't my *neach-gleidhidh* anymore. Best friend? Partner? He was just… *Rory*.

Altrys raised his eyebrows.

"Rory," I murmured. "He… We've been through a lot together. He's probably in the capital right now trying to find out what happened to me."

"He came here with you?"

I nodded.

"Do you love him?"

My cheeks heated. "No, I… He thought he loved me, but its complicated."

Altrys handed me back the knife. "I see."

We were back to an awkward silence. It was probably just my own nervousness and inexperience with people that had me fretting. I was trying, but sometimes words failed to bridge the gap between emotion and reality.

"I'm beginning to doubt everything that's happening here," Altrys admitted.

"What?" My heart twisted and my Fae power stirred.

"Something is in the forest and has altered the Lor'andann's perception," he went on. "I felt it clear as day. What isn't so clear, is the link."

I sighed, my nerves calming. "The spirits are definitely part of it. Being attacked by Chimera is a glaring red flag."

Altrys snorted.

"Those spirits weren't dead things," I added. "They were the same, yet different. They were very much alive, though."

He glanced at me, a hint of wariness flashing in his silver eyes. "You would be the one who knows."

"*Hey*. Are you being a smartarse on purpose? I thought we just bared our hearts to one another and cleared all that up," I fired back.

"I'm just stating the obvious," Altrys replied.

I wasn't sure how to take him now that he knew the truth. He seemed okay with it, then he was almost... worried as if he thought I was going to turn around and suddenly decide I wanted to be evil.

"There's nothing like it in my world," I said thinly. "At least, not that I know of. What could they be?" I absentmindedly poked a stick into the fire, stirring the coals. "You said something about ancient things..."

"Things that are long dead, Elspeth."

I tossed the stick into the fire. "But what if they aren't?"

The *shr'lei* shook his head. "They cannot be brought back."

"Humour me, Altrys."

He sighed and drew his left leg up. Resting his arm on his knee, he scowled at the dark forest. "A tantankai; a parasitic wraith. They have been gone for thousands of years. It cannot be that."

I made a face. "What does it do?"

"It feeds off the guilt and suffering of its intended victim. It grows in strength via its host, then looks to the pain the victim causes those around them."

"Lovely," I drawled.

"They can be created two ways—through flesh or spirit."

"What does that mean?"

"The living creature itself or its resurrected spirit."

"Those orbs…"

"Theoretically, they could be attempts at bringing one back. Or someone could have summoned them to strengthen a live creature."

"If it was a creature, then why hasn't anyone seen it?"

"Because they are made of shadow and rarely move into flesh. Flesh is their weakness." Altrys sighed and shook his head. "This is nonsense. Tantankai are nothing more than myth."

"Okay, so not one of the things." I thought a moment. "What if it's not a curse, but possession?"

"Spirits cannot possess Fae, Elspeth."

"Why not?"

"Because they can't, or at least, not without a great deal of effort. That's besides the point. You said the spirits aren't from the other side."

"Hang on. Don't you think the Chimera would go to a lot of effort to cause unrest here? If Un Alari is so important to their grand plan, wouldn't they do whatever it took to take it?"

Altrys sighed sharply. "Without evidence, all this is speculation. We need to return to the village tomorrow and report what happened here."

"To the Lor'andann? Are you insane?"

"The law demands it."

"Screw the law! You'll out us to the enemy, Altrys, and give away all our advantage. It could jeopardise everything. Then they'll really try to kill us."

"They don't know who you are. That's the ultimate advantage."

"You're counting on that?" I rolled my eyes. "You're really terrible at this detective thing, you know."

"We have to return to Un Alari either way," Altrys told me. "We can't do anything by hiding in the woods."

He was right. The spirits were being watched by the Chimera and so would the village. Going back was our only option if we wanted to figure out what was going on.

Altrys wanted to flush out the Chimera by dropping a bomb on the Lor'andann, but he was risking a bloodbath by doing so. That arrogant twat had the power to end all of us and drive me right into the hands of the enemy.

I huddled into my cloak and rubbed my cold nose against the fabric. It felt like we were about to walk into a trap designed for one person in particular —*Altrys*. I was the anomaly in the scenario, and he was counting on that to save us and the mission. He had more faith in me that I did, that was for sure. At least I was smart enough to figure out what he was planning.

I sighed. The train had already left the station.

"They don't know who I am," I said. "If it comes down to it—"

"Have faith, Elspeth Odhweine. I carry the *tuathade'shri* of the *Shr'lei de Delei'an*."

I snorted and said nothing. Like a pointy brooch was going to save us from the Chimera. *It was the very thing they were using against us.*

"They're going to use your law against us," I murmured. "You do know that, right?"

Altrys nodded. "I know."

"And you're still going to walk in there and shout Chimera at the top of your lungs to the very person who is under their influence." I shook my head. I thought Rory had been rash and over excitable, but

Altrys was a whole new level. "I hope you know what you're getting us into."

"What would you do?"

"Not say anything," I fired back. "Pretend like nothing had happened and continue poking around like secret agents."

"Secret agents?"

"Covert," I told him. "Stealth. Sneaky. Silent."

"I get your meaning," the *shr'lei* said.

"I take it your kind isn't known for their soft touch."

"The *Shr'lei de Delei'an* are the law, Elspeth. If the Lor'andann goes against us, he goes against the queen. It would be an open declaration of war if he were to deny me."

I stared at him, understanding smacking me in the face. "You want him to challenge you."

"Whoever the Chimera agent is, they will believe I'm giving them exactly what they want."

My heart skipped a beat. "And by provoking them, you're forcing the Chimera to reveal their hand."

"We will free Un Alari and the Lor'andann, Elspeth. Do not be afraid. This is how the *Shr'lei de Delei'an* do things." He smirked and tapped the hilt of his sword. "It is as you said… we are not known for our gentle touch."

"And if things go sideways… I am the *Liash li Ashli*."

Altrys lowered his gaze and threw another log onto the fire. "Let's hope it doesn't come to that."

The Lor'andann of Un Alari stared at Altrys and I with unmasked annoyance. His lips puckered like he'd been sucking on a lemon, and he tapped his finger on the arm of his throne, the ring he wore clacking loudly against the wood.

He'd donned a new outfit today—a sliver tunic with gold-armoured scales, and a matching deer antler crown—and his salty wife, Larel, had dressed to match.

"I didn't expect to see you so soon, Altrys, *Shr'lei de Delei'an*," he said, his voice thin. "Is it incompetence that brings you or the inevitable realisation of the devoutness of the people of Un Alari?"

I bit my tongue, struggling against my annoyance. Larel smirked down at us, and I wished I could smack the stupid look right off her face. Who did she remind me of? A rich Stepford wife—no, not quite, though she played the roll well. There was a sharp intelligence in her eyes that seemed absent from her afflicted husband.

"We were attacked in the forest," Altrys said, his voice echoing through the vast hall. "Four masked Fae accosted us during our investigation, and we were forced to defend ourselves."

"Oh my," Larel purred. "You weren't hurt, were you, *Shr'lei*?"

Her fake concern was so sickly-sweet, I nearly vomited.

Altrys's gaze shifted to her as he said, "They were Chimera, my lady."

The Lor'andann paled. "Chimera?"

He nodded. "In your forest, Lor'andann."

"You dare accuse me of conspiring with those fanatics?" He shot to his feet and jabbed a finger at Altrys. "I would never condone such a thing in Un Alari!"

"I never said you did, Lor'andann," Altrys replied smoothly. "I am simply reporting the incident as the law dictates."

"Did you bring proof?" Larel purred. "Until you can procure such evidence, your claims are baseless."

I never thought I'd miss having a smartphone with a fancy camera as much as I did right now. It gave a whole new meaning to the phrase 'pic or it didn't happen'.

"Falsehoods designed to undermine my rule," the Lor'andann ranted. "The rule granted to me by Queen Niarisshia herself!"

"We were attacked in the forest last night," Altrys said, repeating himself. "Whatever is going on here, your full cooperation would be greatly welcomed."

"And I have given it to you!" he cried. "And what have you given me in return, *Shr'lei*? Accusations and heresy!"

"I believe you are in danger, Lor'andann."

"Danger? The only danger here is your arrogance." He waved his hand at the soldiers on either side of the hall. "Guards!"

Altrys bowed low. "That will not be necessary. We both know what will happen if you bear arms against the *Shr'lei de Delei'an*."

"Queen Niarisshia will hear of this," the Lor'andann raged. "I will make sure of it! Get out of my sight before I banish you from Un Alari."

He didn't have to ask me twice. I followed Altrys as he strode from the hall, glad to be out of there. The tension was so thick, it was suffocating.

The moment we were outside, I took a deep breath, filling my lungs with crisp mountain air.

"Well, that went just as I expected," I drawled as the doors slammed closed behind us. *"Like complete shite."*

Altrys didn't reply—a habit I was beginning to find irritating.

"He's paranoid," I said as we made a hasty exit down the street. "He's jumping to the worst possible conclusions."

"Whatever is effecting him, it's getting worse."

"Larel isn't helping. I bet she's in on it."

"Larel?" he scoffed. "She is nothing but a leech on his riches. I've seen her kind before."

A leech on his riches? I snorted, realising it was the Fae equivalent of a gold-digger.

I waited until we'd left the village and were in the woods before replying.

"She plays her part well, Altrys. A little too well, if you ask me." I thought of Owen and how seamlessly he'd worked his way onto the Scottish police force *and* into my life. "I learned the hard way not to take the Chimera at face value. Their manipulations are… Well, they're perfect. I bet you fifty bucks she's in this up to her eyeballs."

I let my Colour ebb forth and cast a weak illusion that would only grow the deeper we ventured into the wilderness.

Altrys grunted. "Fifty bucks? What are bucks?"

The sound of hurried footsteps crunched up the path behind us and Altrys turned, his hand reaching for his sword. When a head of cotton-candy-pink hair emerged from the trees, he sighed sharply.

It was Adrielle.

"What are you doing?" Altrys demanded. "The Chimera are in the forest. If they see you talking to us, they'll kill you."

"Don't worry about that," I told them. "We're concealed by an illusion. We began to fade the moment we walked into the tree line."

Adrielle stared at me in bewilderment.

I screwed up my face. "What? I thought you people knew how to use illusions."

"No," Adrielle said. "Illusions are—"

"Don't tell me," I interrupted, realising I'd put my foot in it. "It's an Unseelie thing. *Perfect.*"

"Who are you?" she whispered, her silver eyes full of suspicion.

"You tell me." I raised my eyebrows. "I thought you could 'see' things."

"*Elspeth*," Altrys warned.

Adrielle blinked, then looked to Altrys. "Your *shride* is Unseelie?"

"I'm no——"

"*Elspeth.*"

Adrielle's brow creased in confusion. Whatever she was here for, it wasn't me. Anyone with eyeballs could see she still had certain *feelings* for Altrys. If they were romantic or simply platonic, who knew but her?

"What are you doing here, Adrielle?" Altrys demanded.

"You provoked the Lor'andann," she hissed.

"I know what I'm doing."

"They will kill you and it will be sooner rather than later. If you die, then you will not stop them. This has all been for nothing."

"Are you so certain we've already failed?"

"Altrys, *please*. I'm trying to help you."

"Did you see it in one of your visions?" He stepped closer to her. "You know I can protect myself. I am a *Shr'lei de Delei'an,* and I've trained for this my entire life. Remember the time your father sent an assassin after me? *What folly that was.*"

"*Altrys.*" Adrielle glanced at me, her expression panicked. It seemed like no one had reported it, and after the song and dance Altrys had given me about the *Shr'lei de Delei'an* being 'the law', no wonder she was pooping her pants right now. She thought I was a *shride*—Altrys's deputy.

"I'm just going to be over there." I squirmed and

began to edge backwards. "Where I can feign selective amnesia."

Moving through the trees, I found myself at the edge of the river. It flowed swiftly, the milky blue water full of sediment from the glaciers twisting through the peaks above Un Alari. This place reminded me of the Rocky Mountains and as I sat on a flat boulder, I could almost imagine that I was back on Earth.

The only thing that brought me back to reality was the low murmuring of Altrys and Adrielle's bickering. It ebbed over the rushing water, but thankfully, I couldn't make out a single word. That was an argument I didn't want to get dragged into if I could help it.

Movement drew my attention downstream and I spotted a group of ten or so women on the opposite bank, washing what looked like bed sheets and clothing in the water. They lifted colourful fabrics out of the current and twisted the excess water out of them before returning them to woven baskets.

They laughed as they worked and began to sing a cheerful tune, their harmonies perfectly arranged. Smiling, I imagined myself amongst them, joining in and enjoying their slow, simple way of life. It was certainly less complicated than the prophecy I faced.

Stupid Chimera.

Altrys had unleashed a dangerous force against us with his bull in a china shop approach, but I wasn't going to sit here and wait for the Chimera to attack

again. If they wanted me, they had to work for it…
and hope I didn't get them first.

Tugging at my hood, I peered at the women
downstream.

And an idea began to form.

12

———

I sensed Altrys returning before I heard him.

Looking up, I saw he had a foul look on his face that signalled his conversation with Adrielle hadn't gone as planned.

"Did you kiss and make up?" I couldn't help myself.

His scowl deepened. "What? *No.*"

"How much does she know?"

He shook his head and sat beside me. "She knows nothing about you, but she will. Now you're on her mind, her visions will eventually reveal it."

"Can I trust her?"

"Adrielle is many things, but she's not a fool. She will see you for who you really are."

I raised my eyebrows. "And who is that?"

"Someone who is opposed to the Chimera."

It wasn't what I was hoping he'd say, but it was good enough. Speaking of…

"I'm not going to sit around and wait for more Chimera ninjas to melt out of the bushes and murder us," I told him. "I'm going to be proactive with my death sentence, thank you very much."

Altrys raised an eyebrow. "And what are you going to do about it, Elspeth, *Shride de Shr'lei*?"

"It could be our last chance at talking to the De'ashlide before the Lor'andann poisons them against us," I replied. "You saw his tantrum back there. Soon he'll have wanted posters stuck up on every available surface. If we're going to do anything about this place, then it has to be now and it has to be quick."

Altrys nodded. "You have a good eye."

"How long do you think we have before we've lost to the Chimera?"

"A day or two. Maybe three if we're lucky."

Great. I'd better get a wriggle on.

I looked downstream at the group of women. They were still washing and had shifted to the next song on their playlist.

"Then I want to start there," I said, nodding towards the Fae.

"The washerwomen?" Altrys asked.

"How different can Fae women be from humans?" I mused. "Women like to gossip, especially when they're working... or bathing... or, pretty much all the time." It was a stereotype I didn't like playing into, but there was truth in it. Men boasted. Women gossiped. There was overlap... *We get the point, Elspeth.* "If I approach them, offer to help, maybe ask for some soap to wash something of my own…"

"You want to go alone?"

"Of course. You're a guy *and* an uptight cop. No one talks smack to cops."

"I have no idea what you just said, but I have the feeling it was an insult."

"It's a reference to a drawback of your profession."

"It doesn't matter," he snorted. "They'll mark you as Unseelie the moment you lower your hood."

"I can use an illusion to mask my hair," I told him. "No one will know."

"No. It's too risky. The last thing I need is to intervene in another hate crime."

"It's not a Fae thing I'm using, so calm your farm, Altrys. No one knows anything about Druid power here. They won't be able to see through it. You can't even sense the illusion on us now."

Altrys blinked. "Calm my farm? I don't—"

"Forget it." I waved my hand at him and knocked my hood off. It was hot and uncomfortable, though the fabric was soft to the touch. I wondered what oddly coloured creature was shaved in order to make it.

"Elspeth…"

"See?" I let my Colour bleed into my hair and the green tresses began to change to an ordinary brown. I knew if he squinted at me in just the right way, with the thought that something wasn't quite right, he'd see right through it.

Altrys did just that. He narrowed his eyes, then opened them again a few times. "I don't like this."

"You know what you're looking for, but they won't." I rose and dusted the dirt off my butt. "I'll find you in the forest. Wait for me."

Altrys sighed, resigning to the fact that I was going to do whatever I wanted, despite his ultimate cop status.

"Here…" He fished around in his little pack and pulled out a folded piece of fabric. He tossed it into a muddy puddle and stomped his boot on it, grinding down his heel. "I can't let you go empty-handed."

I picked up the chestnut fabric with my thumb and forefinger. Luckily for me, it was his spare tunic and not a pair of dirty undies.

"Gee, thanks," I drawled.

"I'll wait for you in the forest." I began to walk down the shore, making for the bridge that spanned the river a few hundred metres past the women.

I'd only gone a few steps before I turned back. "Hey… Will they care that I don't know any Fae?"

"It's not commonly spoken in the capital anymore. They'll just think you're——"

"Slumming it?"

He shrugged. "Whatever that means."

I sighed and waved. "Don't worry, I get it."

"Elspeth?"

I paused and looked back at Altrys.

"Say *E'dreha*, it means greetings."

It seemed like it took forever for me to cross the bridge and return upstream. The whole way, I mulled over what I was going to say to the women. Talking wasn't my strong suit, though I found it incredibly easy with Altrys, despite only meeting two days ago.

Pretend you're a traveller, Elspeth. You're a city girl in the country for the first time. It was an epic cliché, but it seemed like it'd be a universal one.

Walking down the path to the river's edge, I stopped just short of the bank where the women were chattering happily in the sunshine.

A churning sensation began to burn in the pit of my stomach. What was I doing here? How could I ever think I was adjusted enough to approach strangers in an alien world when I couldn't do that in my own?

Sensing someone was lingering, one of the women glanced up. Spotting me, she looked me over and smiled.

She was rather plain, but pretty in her own way— much like I'd been before my hair turned green. Her chestnut hair was twisted into a tight braid that snaked down her back almost to her waist and she bent over the tub full of soap suds, rubbing clothing over a ribbed washboard with an expert hand.

"*E'dreha*," I said, stepping forwards.

"Not from around the Reaches, are you?" she asked, wiping her hands on her apron.

"Is it that obvious?"

She laughed and beckoned for me to approach. "Have you something to wash, dear?"

"Yes, I…" I glanced at the tub. "May I borrow some soap?"

This was greeted with silence, but after a moment, the woman said, "They call me Saria."

"El—" I cleared my throat. "Els."

"Els? That's a cute little name." Her gaze dropped to the knife at my hip. "Do you know how to use that?"

"There's dangers in the world," I murmured uncertainly.

"Yes, I suppose there are." Saria nodded. "What brings you this far north?"

"Adventure."

She laughed and the other women joined in.

"It's always the romance of adventure," one said.

"I'd like to go adventuring," another chimed in, "and leave my lazy husband behind."

"I'd like to see him work a washboard," Saria said. "It'd near break his back!" She held out her hand and wriggled her fingers. "Come, Els. Show me your hands."

I moved closer and sat on a rock beside the tub and held out my hands. She grabbed my wrists and jerked me close and clucked her tongue.

"Smooth as silk, *bashide.* Have you ever worked a day in your life?"

"I've worked enough."

"Well, let's see." Saria handed me a bar of sweet-smelling soap and began to teach me the finer arts of hand washing. Soon, my shoulders ached and Altrys's tunic was full of suds.

"Un Alari is beautiful," I said as I worked. "I've never seen mountains like these."

Saria nodded. "They are ancient, that is known. I hear the capital has its own beauty to rival them."

I shrugged. "Perhaps it's the thrill of a new place."

"Have you ever seen the queen?" one of the other women asked.

"Once," I said, making it up as I went alone. "But it was from far away."

"I hear her hair is made from starlight," another woman gushed. "And her voice carries throughout the capital like music."

"I hear your Lor'andann has his own beauty," I said, attempting to steer the conversation.

Saria snorted and the women fell silent.

I hesitated, my hands slowing against the board. "Did I say something wrong?"

"There are rumours…" Saria murmured.

My eyes widened. "Rumours?"

She nodded. "Apparently, as a young man, the Lor'andann murdered his older brother in a fit of jealousy. His brother was more handsome, skilled, and charismatic, *and* the heir to the lordship of the forests."

I leaned closer. "He wanted to be Lor'andann over his brother?"

"It's merely a rumour, and a nasty one at that," she replied.

"Tell her the story, Saria," a woman said. "Everyone fawns over the Lor'andann and she should know before she pays tribute."

Saria looked at me. "Have you?"

"Paid tribute?" I didn't know what it meant, but I shook my head. Somehow, I didn't think Altrys and I pissing him off counted as tribute.

"Good. You seem like a nice girl, Els. The Lor'andann is difficult to please, but his wife Larel… Her approval is even harder won." She looked me over again. "You are too plain. Not to insult you, dear, but they'd never take you."

Take me? My cheeks heated as I suddenly realised what tribute meant. People offered themselves for threesomes? I felt like throwing up.

Saria and the washerwomen laughed at my reaction.

"She's not paying any tribute any time soon," a woman by the river called out. "I've never seen cheeks so red!"

"Still, tell her the story, Saria."

The De'ashlide looked at me, her smile widening. "The Lor'andann is handsome, that is true, but his brother was fairer still. Tall, strong, with eyes like polished silver, and a voice like the warm rays of the sun. He would have made a glorious Lor'andann. Some say had he lived, he would have even challenged for the hand of Queen Niarisshia herself."

She took the bar of soap from me and flipped over Altrys's tunic, intending to finish for me.

"All men of the Lor'andann lineages are required to pass certain trials before they are found worthy of rule," she went on. "They went out hunting, travelling to the farthest reaches of the woods in a test of honour and strength."

"What were they hunting?" I asked.

"Why, the silver stag of Un Alari, of course!" the women next to me said.

I glanced at the women. "Silver stag?"

"The stag is a great magical beast that roams the remote Reaches," Saria explained. "Its likeness is everywhere you gaze in Un Alari." *And sat atop the Lor'andann's pompous head.* "The trial dictates that the worthy must trap the creature and take its antlers as a prize. They must not kill the stag, lest they curse Un Alari for eternity."

"Did they kill it?" My heart leapt. Maybe this was the curse Altrys had suspected.

Saria shrugged. "What happened out in the wilds is unclear, and none may ever know the truth besides the Lor'andann, but only one brother returned. He carried the antlers of the silver stag and the blood of his brother on his tunic."

The woman next to me leaned close. "People say his brother's remains are hidden in the forest, that's why the spirits are restless. He is angry that he never received a proper burial."

"He was recovered by the guard," Saria told them. "He's buried in the village."

"Maybe it's the stag," I murmured.

The women laughed and I lifted my head.

"Oh no," Saria told me. "It's not the curse that's stirring up the spirits. If the silver stag were dead, Un Alari would have been swallowed up by the ground a long time ago. Here." She handed me the tunic and nodded towards the river. "It's time to rinse the dirt and soap away."

"Then what is making them restless?" I asked as the tunic dripped soap and water on the toes of my boots.

"Sometimes they are restless because they feel ignored," the Fae replied, unperturbed by the goings-on. "They are paid tribute, then they rest once more. It is the way of all things."

Paid tribute? It certainly wasn't the same tribute the Lor'andann and his wife liked, but something else. *The blood on the Lor'andann's tunic.*

I kicked off my boots—I stashed them behind a rock so the De'ashlide wouldn't see they were Earth-made—and waded into the river. As the current tugged at my legs, I held the tunic in the current and thought about the story Saria had told me.

The puzzle pieces were beginning to align… and I wasn't sure I liked where this was going.

I sat with the washerwomen for a while longer before I said my farewells, though I felt a little guilty about deceiving them. They'd welcomed me into their circle without judgement, thinking I was one of them—a De'ashlide. If they'd known I was an Unseelie Shri'danann, I doubt they would have been friendly at all. Perception was everything.

I was on my way back to Altrys when I sensed someone on the path ahead. My Colour lay over me in a protective illusion, though I stepped forwards with caution.

My hand rested on the hilt of my knife, Altrys's damp tunic twisted in the other, and I saw a flash of pink through the trees.

"Elspeth?"

Adrielle sat beside the trail as if she'd been waiting for me since she'd left Altrys earlier.

I glanced over my shoulder, but we were alone. I was also cloaked, so how… "You saw me in your visions, didn't you?"

She nodded. "I knew you'd come this way."

I was obviously going to hear was she had to say, despite not wanting to be drawn into whatever she had going on with her ex, the *Shr'lei*.

"And?" I asked with a sigh.

"It's not because of his oath," she told me, glancing at the tunic.

"Excuse me?"

"It may have begun because of it, his heart is

hardened by the life he was forced into, but it's more than honour."

My brow creased. "I don't understand."

"Our path's will not intertwine, but he will be there," she went on, her silver eyes misting over. "In the darkness you will chose, but beware… *She is not who she seems.*"

"Who?" I resisted the urge to shake her.

Adrielle blinked, her eyes clearing. "I've no control over what I see. I'm simply charged with delivering the message."

"But what does it mean?"

The Shri'danann smiled apologetically. She didn't know, either.

"Once you leave Un Alari, we will never meet again, Elspeth." She raised her hand in farewell. "Until then, *tha sinn còmhla riut.*"

I froze, my heart jerking in my chest. She said— She spoke— Rory said that to me right before we descended into the caves to fight Mindel and the Chimera.

Tha sinn còmhla riut. We are with you.

By the time I'd gathered my wits and my words, Adrielle had already disappeared down the path towards the village.

13

___

I threw the wet tunic at Altrys as I walked into the clearing.

"Did you know the Lor'andann is a filthy pervert?"

He looked up, his lips quirking.

"You knew, didn't you? They thought I was asking about him because I wanted to offer myself as…" I reddened.

"Tribute?"

"*Gross.*"

"I didn't think he was the kind of man you would be attracted to," Altrys said. He stood and threw his tunic over a branch.

I rubbed the heel of my hand over my heart. "Are you being mean on purpose? Because it's wearing thin."

"Are you all right?"

"I'm fine."

Altrys frowned. He didn't believe me, but it didn't matter. I owed him little in the way of explanations about my personal feelings.

"Did you learn anything from the women?" he asked, choosing not to press.

I nodded and told him the story the washerwomen had recounted about the Lor'andann, his brother, and the silver stag, though I didn't mention Adrielle's ramblings. I had the feeling it would only serve to distract Altrys, and we both needed to focus right now.

"The Lor'andann might not be as innocent as we first thought," I said.

"The Chimera likely took advantage of his past pain."

"So, it's a fifty-fifty chance its one of those gross tantankai things or the vengeful spirit of his brother. Either way, it has the Chimera's fingerprints all over it."

"We can do something about the brother," Altrys said. "We should start there."

"And if it's a tantankai?"

"Then we kill it."

"How do we do that?"

"Stabbing usually works."

"But it's a shadow…" I clicked my fingers. "Draw it into the light, then stick it with the pointy end!"

A small smile pulled at Altrys's mouth. I knew he liked me. We worked well together.

"First, the brother," he said. "Can you conceal us

with your Druid illusion again?"

I nodded. "But what about the person behind all this? The Chimera agent?"

"When their plan is foiled, they will reveal themselves," Altrys said. "Then we will strike."

Reaching for my Colour, I let a prism grow before casting it around us. "Don't make eye contact with anyone or they'll see us. Especially not anyone who's looking for us."

"I thought—"

"It's an illusion, not an invisibility cloak," I grumbled. "What about your washing?"

"It'll be here when we get back," he replied. "If not, I'll just get another one."

"*Shr'lei* get a big salary, huh?"

He rolled his eyes. "Let's go. We only have a few hours of sunlight left."

Thankfully, the cemetery was on the outskirts of Un Alari, so we didn't have to walk through the centre of town to find it. It meant less eyes to see through our cloak and even less chances of being discovered by the Lor'andann ordered, Chimera-backed, hitman squad on our tail.

We passed under a stone arch and emerged into another world.

Stone lanterns were packed densely into the clearings amongst the thick woodland. They reminded me a little of the totem poles of the First Nations people of North America. The stone was unadorned with colour, though the elaborate carvings running the length of each made up for it. Some were more detailed than others—a likely sign of wealth and status—and pieced together from different kinds of rock. Hollows housed spaces for candles and other trinkets, and there were several along the taller lanterns while others had none at all.

"What are they? They look like lanterns."

"*Ashlar an lor*," Altrys replied. "A place to honour the dead. The shrines are called *lor'ashlar*."

"Lor… like in Lor'andann?"

"Yes. *Lor* is a way to mark respect of one's name." Like calling someone a Lord or a Lady, I supposed.

My senses lay dormant, telling me that any dead had long departed. No vengeful spirits lingered here… just in the forest.

I told Altrys as much and he grunted, replying that it was his remains that mattered, not where his spirit roamed.

"How do Fae handle burials, anyway?" I asked, looking around at the sea of shrines.

"Our bodies are cleansed by fire so we can return to the air. Our ashes are buried at the base of a *lor'ashlar* to return us to the earth. Once we are free of our bodies, our spirits climb, gathering the wisdom of our life's endeavours before we venture into the next life. Those are represented in the carvings."

"That's beautiful." I studied the *lor'ashlar* as we passed, catching glimpses of the images chiselled into the stones.

"The Fae cherish life as well as death. Spirit is

hallowed here, Elspeth Odhweine."

I couldn't help snorting at this. It felt as if he was taking a shot at me.

Altrys turned. "Elspeth, I didn't mean—"

"I don't like it," I interrupted. "I don't want to be like this. If I could give it back, I would."

He placed a hand on my arm and I tensed, his touch unfamiliar. It wasn't like it was *unwelcome*, I guess I just wasn't used to it.

I narrowed my eyes. "How do we find the right shrine? Look for the tallest and gaudiest?"

Altrys forced a smile and nodded. "The taller a *lor'ashlar* is—"

"The more important they were."

"The more eventful their life was… in relation to how much wealth was left behind for their *lor'ashlar*."

I chuckled. "Same thing, really."

We found a tall *lor'ashlar* set apart from the others on a rise at the back of the cemetery.

It was made up of a dozen tiers of various types of stone, each finely carved with various deeds and exploits. It had to be at least a metre wide and three tall. Most of the other shrines were much slimmer— some hadn't even been a handspan across.

This one was definitely for someone important.

I didn't know much about rocks, but the tiers seemed to be made of bluestone, quartz, granite, and some others I didn't recognise. Limestone, maybe? At the top, was a stag head with twisted and broken antlers, the tips dipped in liquid silver.

"I take it this is his?"

"Yes." Altrys traced his fingers over some glyphs below a hollow stuffed full of candles and jewelled trinkets. "This marks his name and title."

"What was his name?" I wondered.

"His name was Ylyndar."

"Ylyndar," I murmured, trying out the unfamiliar letters. I glanced at the base of the shrine. "How do you tell if his ashes are there?"

"The elements will tell me." Altrys knelt before the shrine and placed his hands onto the grass before it.

I felt the air vibrate softly as he called on his magic. My Colours rippled in response as the ground began to absorb his energy. His ability wasn't all that different from a Druid's really. He could read the currents of nature and help them grow. It wasn't exactly like shooting fireballs out of his hands, but it was still a pretty impressive power to have.

"It's empty," Altrys said, rising. "There's nothing here."

I snapped out of my daze. "What?"

He dusted his palms on his trousers. "It seems the rumours may be true."

"So, what now? We need his remains to help his spirit."

Altrys laughed and raised his eyebrows. "We go into the forest and search for them, that's what."

"Do we have time? I mean, you've seen that forest.

We could be searching for the rest of our lives and not find a single thing."

"Between you and me, I'm sure we can find a way," he told me. "You are skilled in that area, are you not?"

I froze. I'd been so cautious with my Colour it hadn't even crossed my mind. If the Lor'andann's brother was out there wandering between life and death, then I'd be able to find him.

I'd have to Spirit Walk.

"I can ask him," I said, looking to the sky. The shadows were beginning to lengthen. "If he's willing to talk, that is."

"I knew… I…" Altrys seemed dumbfounded by this new revelation. "You can do that? You can go to the next life?"

"Death," I corrected. "The in-between… and yes. I won't do it here, though. If I use my abilities, it may alert the Chimera. They may already know I'm here after…"

Altrys frowned. "Then let's go into the forest. I will protect you." He looked me over. "Though I'm not sure you need it."

Considering I went through the veil body and all, protection was not on the list of priorities, though I'd miss Ignis.

"No, I won't," I told him.

He raised his eyebrows.

"Don't let it dent your pride, Altrys. You'll see why soon enough."

We ventured deep into the wilds, finding a secluded space where I'd be safe to travel through the veil.

The forests surrounding Un Alari were becoming familiar and welcoming, despite the things which lurked in forgotten corners. The more attuned I became with the Fae world, the more I sensed the creatures who called this place home. And more than just the humanoid Seelie and Unseelie, and the animals that were so similar to the ones on Earth, that lived here.

Spirits, elementals, sprites, and other creatures dwelt in all parts of the land—from the mountains to the valleys, from the ice to the sand.

I hoped I'd be able to keep the black sun from rising long enough to see some of them.

"Here," I said, beckoning to Altrys. "This is as good a place as any."

"What do I do?"

"You? Nothing." I smiled as I reached for the veil and my Colour. "Just wait and keep your eyeballs peeled."

He screwed up his face. "Eyeballs?"

"Just keep watch." The cool brush of death chilled my cheeks and I turned, stepping over the threshold to the other side.

The grey mists rose and the currents tugged at my ankles, attempting to draw me into the stream of souls bound for the next life.

"I'm looking for Ylyndar," I called into the grey. "Ylyndar of Un Alari."

The forest shimmered around me and I looked over my shoulder. Altrys was gone, but he was still firmly in life. He wouldn't be here, even as an echo.

"Ylyndar of Un Alari," I said again. "I'm here to help you, *Ylyndar of Un Alari.*"

I walked a little deeper, searching for signs of his binding, but it was his spirit that found me instead.

A man walked towards me, brought forth by my calls as if he were waiting for someone to come. He was devoid of colour and everything about him was etched in shades of grey.

Ylyndar.

The resemblance to his brother was uncanny, though he had a more masculine edge to his features. His long hair was twisted back at the sides with thick braids, much like the ones Altrys wore, though more care had gone into keeping Ylyndar's dreadlock-free.

His spirit had chosen to remain in the simple clothes he'd likely worn when he was hunting the silver stag—trousers, boots, and a loose tunic. A bow was slung over his shoulder, the string held taught across his chest, and a quiver of arrows sat on his back, the fletched ends sticking up over his left-hand side.

Ylyndar's spirit form swirled, the currents viciously tearing at his ankles, but no matter how strong they were, he would not move. He was bound.

He sensed my approach and I stopped, feeling his anger rise.

"Unseelie." He turned sharply. "You are one of *them*."

His gaze burned into mine and I felt the threads anchoring him to the world of the living. They were wound so tight, I knew I wouldn't be able to break them without some serious magic.

"No," I said with a shake of my head, "I am not one of them. I am not Chimera."

"You are *Unseelie*. You are in death."

"It's not my Unseelie magic that helps me walk the currents of death. I come from elsewhere. I am made of other magic, too."

His lip curled. He knew he couldn't touch me here, but how much he knew about what I could do to him was unknown.

"Your kind bound me," he hissed. "I was already lost, but now I am trapped for eternity."

Of course, the Chimera were Unseelie, but it wasn't an all-encompassing umbrella for the Dark Fae. I did not have grey skin and pointy teeth. I didn't need to use illusion to look human, just like many other Unseelie Fae. Who knew what made the Chimera change? Who knew anything for sure…

"That's why I'm here, Ylyndar," I said. "We're trying to free you… and your brother, the Lor'andann."

This made him pause. "We?"

"I'm helping a *Shr'lei de Delei'an*."

"The Queen's Blades have come?" His frown deepened. "Then it is dire indeed."

"I don't understand what it is to be Unseelie," I told him. "I never knew what I was for a long time, but what I do know is that the Chimera cannot be allowed to manipulate you or your brother. If Un Alari falls, then the path to the capital is open. It will begin here, Ylyndar. Please, let us help you."

He stood frozen, appearing more like a marble statue than a spirit. I should really start calling death the Greylands. I let out a sigh, and it was enough to stir Ylyndar.

"Dark forces swirl around him," he said. "He cannot escape, not without help."

"Forgive me for saying this, but aren't you the one bound to him?"

Ylyndar shook his head. "No, not quite. I never intended to be vengeful, but because of my brother… What he did caused me to linger." He looked around the grey world, his eyes sad. "It left my spirit open to be manipulated by others."

"Manipulated? How?"

"Forbidden magic," he replied. "Dark, terrible, and ancient."

"So, someone is forcing you to haunt your brother?"

"Yes." He began to reach a hand towards me, then stopped, his expression falling. "His pain and my spirit… They——"

"Created an opening for the Chimera," I finished for him.

"I don't know who is doing this. I don't know if it is the Chimera. I cannot see into life anymore."

"Ylyndar, your remains weren't buried with your *lor'ashlar*. That's why we think you're still lingering."

"What?" He shook his head and fisted his hands into his hair. "We fought, but he's never… He'd…"

I hated to ask him, but we were running out of time. "What happened to you the day you died? Where did you fall?"

Ylyndar took a deep breath and let his hands fall to his sides.

"My brother was jealous," he told me. "He wanted to be the Lor'andann more than I. It was my duty to serve and so it would have been. Honour and tradition bound us to both enter the forests and hunt the *Un Fall'an*."

"What happened?" I asked. "When you found the silver stag?"

"It charged him," Ylyndar choked out. "I-I pushed him out of the beast's path, I lifted my sword, and it struck me. At first, I was well. Wounded, but well."

"Who was the one who…?"

"I felled the *Un Fall'an*," he replied, "leaving it stunned as I severed the antlers. I—" He hesitated, his brow creasing. "We fought, I think. Yes, we fought. He saw his chance and he took it. I was wounded and I couldn't… My brother strung his bow and put an arrow through my heart." Ylyndar choked back a sob and pressed the heel of his palm against his chest. "I fell and he left me there. He took the antlers and left me there to die." His spirit started to shudder, and a wound opened up over his heart. Grey blood seeped through his tunic and began to drip down his front. "He left me to die. *His own brother.*"

"I'm sorry," I murmured. "I'm so sorry."

"What for?" He was whispering now, shock setting in. "Was power more important than the love of a brother? I would have… I would have done *anything* for him."

"Where did you fall?"

He looked up, his expression twisted by grief.

"Please, Ylyndar. If we burn your remains and bury them at your *lor'ashlar*, then you will be free."

He nodded. "I know, but…"

"Show me."

"I can't go back."

"You can if you want to save Un Alari."

Tears began to fall down his cheeks and he looked up at the mountain. He lifted his shaking hand and pointed towards the nearest peak.

I held out my hand. "*Show me.*"

His fingers were slick with blood as he twisted them with mine, but I didn't feel his touch at all. His silver eyes shone within the currents and he showed me where his body lay.

A hidden glade beside a gushing waterfall. Slick rocks, mossy trees, and thick ferns. The base of a great tree, whose roots grew up and out of the earth in an elaborate maze. The Lor'andann had left his murdered brother there, never to be laid to rest.

"Thank you," I murmured. "I promise I will do everything I can to make sure you are laid to rest. You will be free to leave this place and move onto the next."

Ylyndar looked at me, his hand slipping form mine. "What is your name?"

"Elspeth," I told him. "I am Elspeth Odhweine."

"Odhweine," he whispered as he began to fade. "I met a man once whose name was Odhweine…"

I opened my mouth, but the words died in my throat as I fell back through the veil. I landed on my knees, gasping for breath.

Altrys was beside me in an instant. "Elspeth, what is it?"

"H-he knew my father."

"Your father?"

I nodded. I knew if we set Ylyndar free, I'd never be able to ask him what he knew. Did he know my mother? It was selfish, but I found myself considering going back.

"He showed me where his remains are," I said instead. A whole world was at stake. Now wasn't the time for personal gains. "The place where the Lor'andann murdered his brother."

Altrys sensed my hesitation. "Are you sure?"

"Yes. We have no time." I grabbed his hand and phased.

14

ltrys wasn't a fan of phasing.

Ylyndar had shown me where to find his remains, and I was able to take us there in a blink of an eye.

I stood to the side as Altrys performed a burial rite, burning the bones into ash, his magic feeding the flames which consumed the last thing binding Ylyndar to the living. All that was left to do was return him to his *lor'ashlar* so he could begin his long-delayed journey to the next life.

Altrys didn't like it, but I phased us there too, and once it was all said and done, we stood side by side before the shrine, staring up at the night sky.

"It's such a sad story," I murmured.

"But not a surprising one," Altrys countered. "Ylyndar would have made a good Lor'andann."

"But we have another problem."

"The anchor is gone."

I sighed. "But the curse hasn't lifted."

The *shr'lei* looked at me with raised eyebrows. "We haven't even had the chance to see if it is so. Dawn is still a few hours away, Elspeth."

"Ylyndar led me to believe that he wasn't the only thing binding the Lor'andann. His murder left a stain on the Lor'andann's soul which allowed other darker magic to take hold. Ylyndar was the anchor, but——"

"He is no longer needed," Altrys finished.

"It *is* a tantankai," I said. "They couldn't summon it without binding Ylyndar's spirit. That's what people have been seeing in the forest. Those orbs aren't elementals, they're the tantankai… and they're bewitching the people too, aren't they?" That's why no one seemed to care about the Lor'andann's crazy. "The whole of Un Alari…"

His silence was all the confirmation I needed.

"I don't know what to do," he admitted quietly. "We're running out of time… and welcome. My powers as *shr'lei* are at breaking point. If we march into Un Alari and start throwing around accusations——"

I snorted. "Now you worry about that?"

"If the Chimera are powerful enough to summon a tantankai…"

"We have to kill it, Altrys. We have to take the risk. You know it's our last chance."

His jaw tensed. "It's bound to the Lor'andann.

We'd have to sever it from his body and they're not going to just let us in. It means breaking into his house past all those guards *and* the Chimera agent."

"If we're caught, you can act as if you're there to stop me," I went on. "You're a shr'lei, I'm Unseelie. They'll believe you."

"*No*. You'll be thrown into the dungeons and executed."

"I'll be able to phase out of there before that." Besides, I had a prophecy protecting me. I wouldn't die in Un Alari; Adrielle had foreseen my journey past this place, but Altrys's fate was uncertain. All that helped him was his shiny badge and I intended to make sure it saved him.

He scowled and turned away, ever the stubborn male.

I grabbed his arm. "Altrys, I'm right about this."

His silver eyes flashed. "How can you be certain?"

"The moment I touch him, I can force his truth. If he's possessed by that thing, I'll know immediately."

"Force his truth?"

"All are judged when they stare into the eyes of death."

"You want to use your magic?" he hissed.

"It's worth the risk."

"Worth alerting every Chimera to your arrival?" He shook his head. "*No*."

"I've used my magic four times. I got away with it the first time, but tonight? They're coming, Altrys. We need to save Un Alari now or not at all. I'm prepared to do whatever it takes to stop the Chimera. The question is, are you?"

Altrys hissed and turned towards the village. He wasn't used to deferring to someone else, let alone being at a loss as to what to do. That I was the *Liash li Ashli* was just icing on the cake.

"Don't forget what Adrielle said," I told him. "It will begin in—"

Altrys spun towards me and grasped my face. Before I knew what was happening, he kissed me. *Hard.*

It was the kind of kiss out of a movie or a romantic novel. Open-mouthed, searing in all the right places, and toe curling. A million thoughts ran through my mind, but I couldn't settle on just one. His touch was… His touch…

Finally, he pulled away, his hands falling from my face, and all he could say was, "Let's go."

The Lor'andann's house was attached to the hall where we'd previously had both audiences with him.

Un Alari was still asleep and clad in shadow, save for the guards posted outside the one place we needed to go. There were only two of them, but there'd be more around the perimeter and inside. The Chimera wouldn't let their most important asset go unprotected, and we had to be prepared for a major response if things went sideways.

Altrys and I moved down the street, keeping to the darkness as much as we could, even though my Colour concealed us. We skirted the building, scouting the doors and windows, counting guards as we went. There were at least a dozen outside.

At the rear of the building was what looked like a servant's entry. It was guarded on the outside by two armoured Fae men, but their attention seemed a little lax. The door was partially open, the crack letting dim light out onto the stoop, and they either didn't care or hadn't noticed.

Altrys tapped me on the arm and pointed at the door, a questioning expression on his face. *Can we get in there unseen?*

I nodded and pressed my finger to my lips. *Quietly.*

Getting past them and into the house was surprisingly easy. My Druid abilities were foreign here, and the Fae didn't know we were even there as we slipped past, completely concealed.

Altrys remembered the 'no eye contact' rule as we squeezed through the opening, our footsteps silent, but at the last second, the door creaked and the guards turned.

The one on the left said something in Fae, the words unfamiliar.

For a tense moment, Altrys and I stood frozen in the hallway, sure they'd seen us… but the guard simply closed the door.

I heaved a sigh of relief and nudged Altrys with my elbow. We had to keep moving.

At the end of the hall was a set of stairs. Keeping our eyes and ears open, we climbed them to the next level of the house.

The next storey was more opulent, lush rugs covered the wooden floors and paintings and banners depicting the silver stag hung in regular intervals on the walls. Marble sculptures stood on pedestals in little alcoves before tall windows that looked out onto the manicured gardens at the rear of the building.

Totally posh, like something out of a sixteenth-century French chateau, except with more flowery garlands and deer.

There was no light here, save for the glow that ebbed in through the windows. The carpets muffled our footsteps as we worked our way through the house, searching for the Lor'andann's chambers.

Footsteps sounded from ahead and around the corner while a warm glow began to pierce the shadows. I pulled Altrys into an alcove just as a pair of armoured guards turned down the hallway. They wouldn't have seen us, but the hall wasn't wide enough for us to slip past them. The illusion would have faltered the moment they did.

I pressed against Altrys, squeezing into the tight spot. Looking up at him, I was suddenly aware of how close we were. His mouth was an inch from mine and his eyes—

The oblivious guards brushed past us as we stared at one another, then they rounded the corner.

"C'mon," I whispered, edging backwards.

Altrys stepped out into the hallway and we edged towards the main section of the house. Around the corner were two doors. The first led to a bathroom unlike anything I'd ever seen outside a fantasy television show. The Fae didn't have traditional plumbing—it was all buckets, open fireplaces, and metal baths.

The silver stag motif and woodsy garlands continued here, too. It would have been a perfect place to have a bubble bath, but that wasn't what we were here for.

I closed the door and followed Altrys down the hall where he edged open the second door, his senses guiding him to our target.

A bedroom lay within, furnished with more lavish touches than I had time to take in, because we'd found him.

The Lor'andann was in his bed fast asleep, unaware he had guests. He was alone and without a tribute harem, thank goodness—though the bed was certainly big enough for all manner of grossness. I thought it curious that he didn't sleep with his wife and perhaps it was another clue, or maybe the Fae just simply did things differently.

His hair was splayed out across the crimson silk pillows like he was some kind of Sleeping Beauty, and I found myself wondering why we were saving him at all. He'd murdered his brother for power and basked in his arrogance like a marinade. To be honest, it felt like we were choosing the lesser of two evils.

A grand bedhead towered up the wall, the wood paneling carved with images of his glorious hunt for the silver stag. It was inset with gold and silver while jewels glittered in the soft candlelight. Ylyndar was nowhere to be seen, but I wasn't surprised.

"This might get messy," I whispered to Altrys. "Be ready."

"Do what you need to." The *shr'lei* nodded and stationed himself at the door.

I climbed onto the bed, creeping across the expanse to where the Lor'andann lay. The black sun stirred inside me, anticipating what I was about to do. It was excited to be put to use, hoping that I'd finally set it free.

Pushing Altrys out of my mind, I straddled the Lor'andann and slapped my hand over his mouth. His eyes flew open and he began to struggle, but my power forced him down.

His eyes focused on mine and I felt the familiar buzz of the veil creeping into my fingertips. My vision blurred and colour began to fade into the muted tones of the Greylands.

We were on the precipice of life and death.

"Tell me your truth, Lor'andann," I murmured, drawing him forwards. It was so easy now that I was in the Fae world; it took no effort at all and nothing stirred. There was no wind tearing the room into a wild tornado. There was no pain in the Lor'andann's eyes. There was just his truth… as he knew it.

I peeled my fingers away from his mouth and leaned close. *"Tell me."*

"I killed him. I did it," the Lor'andann rasped. "I left him there to rot. The perfect son was not so perfect anymore. No one would cast me aside ever again. I am the Lor'andann of Un Alari. *It's what I deserve.*"

"Tell me something I don't know, Lor'andann," I said, drawing his truth closer to the surface. "Tell me about the Chimera."

"*Chimera.* They are here."

"How are they controlling you?"

"*Ylyndar.*"

"We set Ylyndar free," I told him.

His eyes widened. "The spirits. My knife! I need my knife!"

The Lor'andann began to thrash, the hold over him struggling against my power. It didn't want to reveal itself, which meant it wasn't going to go down without a fight.

"Lor'andann," I said, but he pushed me off with a burst of unexpected strength and I rolled across the bed and onto the floor.

Altrys rushed forwards, just in time to see the Lor'andann's shadow rear up, its mouth opening in a silent scream of anger.

Altrys cursed in Fae and unsheathed his sword. *"You were right."*

The tantankai sank back into the Lor'andann's shadow and the Fae sat up, his expression twisting. He looked positively demonic in the candlelight, his silver eyes misting over.

I stood, my heart beating wildly in my chest. *A beast of shadow…*

"You're being controlled by a tantankai," Altrys said, circling the bed. "A tantankai summoned by the Chimera."

"We're here to free you," I said, drawing my knife.

"A tantankai?" He laughed and spread his arms wide, showing off the dozens of cuts sliced into his flesh. "I am the vessel for the elementals of Un Alari! There are no Chimera here!"

"The wraith has taken your mind, Lor'andann," Altrys said in an attempt to break through. "The pain binds you. It keeps you in its thrall the more you bleed. Can't you see?"

"I can see clearly for the first time in my life," he said as he rose. He stood in the centre of the bed and leapt into the air, landing on the floor, driven by the wraith possessing his soul.

His shadow writhed, his arms grew, and his head elongated, growing two sets of horns that looked like a demonic crown. It was bound tightly to the Lor'andann, his movements echoing the tantankai's as he looked between Altrys and I, choosing which one of us would be his first target.

As it turned out, that target was me. The *Liash li Ashli.*

I called on every piece of training I'd ever had as the tantankai lunged. Jaimie's wisdom when it came to punching someone's lights out. Vanora's stealth tactics. Darby's spiritual strength. Delilah's earthly wisdom. Osna's infallible aim with her stick. Rory's 'laugh in the face of danger' approach. And Ignis's selfless bravery.

I flipped my knife in my hand and ducked under the Lor'andann's flailing arms. Then I used the coiled strength in my upper body to ram the end of the hilt underneath his chin. His teeth clacked together, and his flight was cut off as abruptly as it had begun.

The Lor'andann fell to his knees and gasped as the tantankai attempted to tear away from its host's body. The Fae's back arched as his mouth gaped in a silent cry of agony, the shadow writhing on the wall terrifying in its monstrosity.

Altrys didn't hesitate.

He thrust his sword downwards, the blade passing beside the Lor'andann, leaving his mortal body unharmed. But in the shadows, etched by the candlelight, it sliced through the creature's chest and pierced its heart.

The Lor'andann screamed as the wraith began to disintegrate, the sound of his cries echoing through the house.

"*Altrys*," I said, holding out my hand. Now we'd banished the wraith—I knew we were never going to do this quietly. We had to get out of here before they found us.

Altrys turned and reached out towards me, but his gaze slid past to the open door.

We weren't alone.

I turned to see Larel standing in the doorway, her mouth dropping open as the last of the tantankai dissolved.

"Larel," Altrys began, but she ignored him; instead, she rushed to the Lor'andann's side.

She caught him before he crumpled to the floor, cradling his head against her chest. Stroking his hair, she muttered into his ear, then looked up at us.

Her expression was pure rage as she shouted, "Guards!"

"Larel, he was possessed by—"

"Assassins! You tried to murder the Lor'andann!" she shrieked as several armoured guards ran into the room. "Arrest them! *Arrest them!*"

I backed away, tightening my grip on the hilt of my knife.

"Drop your weapon, *shr'lei*," the senior guard commanded. "You too, *shride*."

Altrys swore and threw his sword at the guard's feet.

"You're making a mistake." I shook my head. "We can still—"

"Elspeth, it's over," Altrys said. "Give them your knife."

I swore in Gaelic and threw my knife down with a scowl. I could kill them all if I chose. All I had to do was—

No. I'd never let the black sun win, no matter what.

I lowered my gaze to where the Lor'andann lay shivering in Larel's arms and I knew.

It was her… and now we were screwed.

15

———

The dungeon was as putrid as I expected it to be, maybe even worse.

Altrys and I were shoved into the darkest cell, our belongings taken, our cloaks ripped from our shoulders, and metal collars forcefully wrapped around our necks.

The door slammed shut, the sound of metal clanging against metal ringing out into the darkness. We were left without a light, save for a small slit at the top of the back wall. I was just tall enough to see out, but there was nothing interesting to see... unless you call the muddy alley behind the guardhouse interesting.

Silence fell around us and my senses found nothing of significance. We seemed to be the only ones here, which meant it was safe to talk.

"It's her," I said to Altrys. "The Chimera agent is Larel."

"Perhaps."

"She saw you kill the tantankai and accused us anyway. It wasn't grief, Altrys. It was her taking advantage."

The door to the dungeon opened and I fell silent, tensing as I saw Larel stride towards us. *Speaking of the devil.*

She was dressed in her floor-length, black, armoured dress, a dainty silver deer antler crown atop her evil head. Holding up her hand, the guards who accompanied her remained at the far end, well out of earshot.

Larel stood before the bars to our cell and regarded us with annoyance.

"The Lor'andann lives," she said coolly.

"What a shame," I drawled. "You were poised to take over his rule. Without a child, there was no one else to become Lor'andann. That's how it was supposed to go, wasn't it?"

"You speak out of turn for a *shride*," she said. "But you're not a *shride*, are you? You are nothing more than Unseelie filth."

"Just as you're not Larel of Un Alari," Altrys replied.

The Fae's lips curled into a sly smile. "The arrival of the *Shr'lei de Delei'an* was unforeseen, but rest assured, the person responsible for the false reports will be joining you tomorrow. Your plot to overthrow the Lor'andann of Un Alari has been foiled."

I curled my hands around the bars, wishing I

could throttle her right then and there. The black sun stirred, pleased with my reaction. It wanted to do more than choke her.

"You are clever, Larel," Altrys said, "but not clever enough."

Larel smiled, her eyes full of triumph. She had us in the palm of her hand and all she had to do was close her fingers around us and squeeze.

"You have merely caused a delay in my plans," she purred. "The damage is reparable. My husband is unwell, and in a few days, he will be returned to his throne."

"Returned to his place as your self-harming Chimera puppet," I snarled.

"At noon, the people of Un Alari will gather in the square," she continued, ignoring me. "There, they will find a wooden platform with a block stained with the blood of traitors, murderers, and thieves. Here, you will both find your final death. There will be no fire to cleanse your remains. There will be no *lor'ashlar* waiting to carry you to the stars. There will be nothing but eternal suffering for what you have done. Your attempt to assassinate the Lor'andann of Un Alari will be answered with death."

I snorted and leaned against the bars. "And what will be waiting for *you* in death, Larel? When you are judged, what will they say about the ancient evil you summoned to possess the Lor'andann?"

"Nothing." Her silver eyes flashed with hatred. "They will say nothing, for they will never admit how he gained power here. The Chimera will restore Un Alari and lead this world onto a path of glory."

I laughed and glanced at Altrys. "Do you hear this? She actually believes the Chimera want peace and prosperity for all." I turned back to the Fae and stared at her, trying to see if I looked on her true face or it lay hidden beneath a glamour of false beauty. When her skin rippled, I smirked. *There it was.* "Utter desolation. That's what your precious fanatics want for this world. They will strip the beauty out of every living creature, they will drain the magic from the elementals, they will bring agony and suffering to all people. They will burn this world to the ground so they can remake it anew. If you help them, Larel, you will be responsible for mass genocide. Now tell me… when you stand before death itself, how will you be judged?"

Larel listened to me with a frozen expression. She neither smiled nor frowned, she barely blinked.

Finally, she said, "The world must die in order to be reborn from the ashes. When the black sun rises, death will choose the hand of fate. When the *Liash li Ashli* returns, the Chimera will rise."

I smiled. She didn't know she spoke to her precious 'god'. Larel was going to have a rude awakening when we stood on that fancy wooden platform at noon.

We stared at one another, Altrys forgotten behind us.

"Did you have the face of a monster before?" I asked. "Or did they make you this way?"

Larel snarled and strode away, the guards at the end of the dungeons snapping to attention at her approach.

"Noon," she called, her voice echoing off the stone. "At noon you will die and none of this will matter."

The door boomed shut, closing off the sound of Larel's final exit from the guardhouse, but all I could think about was Adrielle's visions. *It will begin in Un Alari...*

The last trickle of sand was running through the hourglass and it would take a miracle to stop the Chimera now. We had hours until the executioner's axe came for Altrys's neck. I could only hope that the Lor'andann recovered in time to see his wife's treachery and free us... but deep down, I knew that was never going to happen.

"At least we know one of us isn't destined to die here," Altrys said, echoing my thoughts.

"I can get us out," I murmured, turning away from the bars. "In the blink of an eye, we could be in the forest. Now that I know Un Alari, I can phase."

Altrys tugged at his metal collar. "While we wear these, magic is impossible."

I didn't know if I should tell him the collar was nothing more than an annoying weight around my neck. It might offend him.

He leaned back against the wall and slid down,

settling in for the remaining hours. Patting the space next to him, he said, "Sit down, Elspeth. Pacing will do us no good."

Sighing, I sat beside him.

"Ylyndar knew your father," he murmured.

"Me knowing my mother isn't high on our list of priorities right now," I drawled. "Saving Un Alari is a little more urgent, don't you think?"

Altrys smiled and let out a little sigh.

"What?" I demanded.

"I knew I was right saving you that day."

"That day? It was like three days ago, Altrys. It still counts as current events."

"I mean to say, it feels as if I've known you forever, Elspeth Odhweine."

I froze, my eyes searching his. I felt the same way, but I didn't understand why. It just *was*.

"Tell me a story," I murmured. "Otherwise, I'm going to go crazy."

Altrys raised his eyebrows. "A story?"

"What about the one with the assassins? It seems relevant."

He laughed and ran his hand over his face.

"We both know how it ends, so there's an HFN ending, right?"

"HFN?"

"Happy for now."

He smiled and tapped the scar on his jaw. "It was nearly an unhappy ending."

"Chicks dig scars."

His lips twitched.

"So, once upon a time…" When he tilted his head in a silent question, I added, "Where I come from all fairy stories start with 'once upon a time'."

"Well then. Once upon a time…" he began, then fell into a serious tone. "Adrielle's family is well-respected in the capital and as a Shri'danann of high birth, she was destined for greater things than a low born *Shr'lei*. Especially one who is half De'ashlide. I have some magic at least, but not the right appearance." He glanced at me. "Are you sure you want to hear this?"

"Sure, why not. I have a terrible destiny that tears me apart from everyone I care about, too. Maybe I've finally found something I can relate to."

"You don't—"

"What happened next?"

Altrys grimaced and leaned his head back against the uneven wall. "She dared to love me, and I dared to let her." He was silent for a long time before he continued, "We stole away on many occasions. We could only meet in secret, for it would mean my death if we were discovered. She was destined for another as her birth dictated. A profitable match, and a powerful one, too."

"An arranged marriage? They have those here?"

"Yes. The morning Adrielle was to marry her betrothed, we decided to leave everything behind. Me, my calling as a *Shr'lei*, and her, her family and everything that went with it." It seemed romantic, running away so they could be together forever. "But it wasn't long before they picked up our trail. Assassins attacked us in the middle of the night. They dragged me away from our camp and we fought. I had a sword at my throat when Adrielle came running out of the forest. She… she begged for my life." He sighed, pausing for a moment. "They offered my life in exchange for leaving her. I refused, but Adrielle… She was the one who begged me to accept."

"And did you?"

He nodded. "But she never did. Now Adrielle is simply Adrielle at the edge of the world, while I am Altrys, *Shr'lei de Delei'an*."

She lost everything to save him—her family, her reputation, her wealth. She'd even lost her name. If that wasn't true love, I didn't know what was.

Altrys seemed to read my expression with crystal-clear accuracy. "Our love wasn't real, Elspeth. It was the fantasy of misguided youth. It was a fleeting moment in time that almost cost us everything." He looked away. "It wasn't true."

"It was true for her."

"No," he murmured. "Adrielle had seen what would happen to her if she married that man and she knew she needed a way to escape. Her father was cruel and arrogant. Her betrothed was of the same ilk. If she had gone home, then her life would have been… She could never go home."

"Are you saying…" My heart swelled.

"Her love was true, but…" He lowered his head. "In the end, she was willing to throw it away."

She'd used him.

I wanted to reach out and comfort him, but I couldn't find the courage. The echo of his kiss still played across my lips and after that… There was nothing I could say. Larel had implied that Adrielle would be on that platform tomorrow, facing the same axe that would take him.

Did he want me to save her? After seeing them together and knowing the risk she'd taken reporting the Chimera activity in Un Alari, the answer was yes. Adrielle was just a victim of her circumstances. If she didn't care for him, she wouldn't have saved his life all those years ago.

Altrys looked up and stared straight ahead, his expression closed. "Whatever comes for me at noon, I will face with the honour of a true *Shr'lei de Delei'an*. I do not fear it."

"Don't," I whispered.

"Elspeth, you mustn't feel responsible for this."

"No, it's…" I wiped at my tears. "I'll feel it, Altrys. When you die, I will feel your soul pass through the veil. I don't think I could… I—"

He leaned against me and cupped my cheek. Soothing his thumb across my damp skin, he sighed and let me go.

"I'm sorry," he told me. "I should never have kissed you like that."

My fingers ached and I wriggled away from him.

"I wouldn't worry. I've never been in love, so I wouldn't know how it feels."

His expression didn't change.

I wanted to know how it felt. "Altrys…"

He shook his head.

"It's okay," I told him, my heart cracking. "You think you're going to die and I'm clueless. What a pair we make."

There was nothing to say, so we waited in silence as the dawn moved into morning, the light spreading across the cell. Soon, it was murky rather than dingy, not that it was much of an improvement.

"I'm not going to let you or Adrielle die, Altrys," I murmured. "I won't allow it."

"I have the feeling that even you don't have that power, Elspeth."

I tugged at my metal collar. "How much do you want to bet on it?"

He glanced at my neck, then back at me. He understood.

"There's time for one last play, Altrys, *Shr'lei de Delei'an*," I whispered. "What will it be?"

"If we want to foil Larel's plans, the people need to see her for what she really is. They need to see the true face of the Chimera and the power of the *Liash li Ashli* in the guise of good. They need to see you, Elspeth."

"If I stand up there as death, I will be declaring open war, Altrys. *I can't.*" I grasped his hands in mine. "I can take us away from here."

"If we stay, I'm dead. If we leave, I'm merely delaying it. The shr'lei will hunt me for my indiscretion and execute me for it. They won't see the lie. I won't follow the same path." He touched his finger to his scar. "I cannot."

"But—"

"Our laws are simple. Elspeth. They will see what Larel wants them to see unless we change the narrative. The tantankai is dead and with it, the magic binding Un Alari. They must see you."

We must trick the trickster.

My heart sank and I found myself thinking of my father. After everything he'd sacrificed to keep me from the Chimera, here I was, playing right into their hands. He'd died to protect me from them, but our predicament made it seem as if it were inevitable.

I'm sorry, Dad. I didn't want it to be this way.

The *Liash li Ashli* had to announce her arrival. It was the only way to save them all.

I lowered my gaze and tightened my grip on Altrys hands.

"*Tha me còmhla riut,*" I whispered.

"What does that mean?"

I swallowed hard and gathered my courage. "*I am with you.*"

16

They came for us just before noon.

Guards forced black hoods over our heads, the fabric too thick to allow enough air through. My breath was short as I gasped, and I began to sweat almost instantly.

We were dragged out of the cell and up the stairs, no thought given to our comfort. I stubbled, tripping so often I was clipped on the back of the head with an angry armoured fist.

My power stirred, sensing death as we were led blindly through the streets.

Finally, my boots stomped on a set of wooden stairs and the presence of a thousand souls brushed up against my senses. We'd arrived and there was a hungry audience waiting for the spectacle of the century.

The hood was wrenched off my head and I sucked in lungfuls of cool, clear air. The moment my green hair was revealed, the sound of shocked gasps turned my head.

The whole population of Un Alari was crammed into the square before the wooden platform on which we stood. There were so many Fae, they poured back into the alleys and lanes; some even leaned out of windows of the surrounding buildings, trying to get close enough to see what was happening.

When they realised Altrys was also in chains, low murmurings began to spread.

My gaze fell to the large wooden block in the centre of the platform and dread began to pool in my stomach. There was a dip in the middle large enough for a person to lay their head and neck, and a woven basket before it. Dark brown stains marred the polished wood and I looked to the man standing at the side… and the long-handled axe in his hands.

My neck began to ache at the same time Larel ascended the stairs, the guard detail shadowing her thundering stride onto the platform. She was wearing the same black gown covered in silver scales, her head adorned with the antler crown that matched the Lor'andann's.

She stood before the people of Un Alari, every part the queen she'd styled herself to be.

"Un Alari is under attack," Larel cried, her voice silencing the chattering before her. "These two Fae came to us claiming to work for Queen Niarisshia. A Shr'lei de Delei'an and his Shride… but they *lied!*"

As I scanned the crowd, I recognised Saria and

some of the washerwomen I'd spoken to at the river. I wished I could explain, because their faces said it all —they believed I'd betrayed them.

"Last night, they were caught attempting to assassinate your Lor'andann!" Larel continued. "They tried to murder him in the name of evil! They are false! They are agents of the enemy! They are *Chimera!*" People began to talk louder, and a few shouted things in Fae. I didn't understand what they said, but I had a vivid imagination. "For their crimes against Un Alari, they are sentenced to death by beheading. But…" She raised her hand and gestured.

A scuffle broke out on the side of the platform as two guards wrestled with a third hooded figure.

"This woman was caught conspiring," Larel proclaimed. "There will be no mercy for those who dare to threaten the Lor'andann and his rule."

They dragged them to the block and tore off the hood, revealing a shock of pink hair that sent a gasp through the assembled villagers.

The guards threw Adrielle down onto the platform. She landed hard on her knees, crying out in pain as her head was shoved towards the block.

Altrys struggled against the guard who held him and the crowd called out objections.

"In the name of the Queen, for the crime of conspiracy against the crown, I sentence the Fae known as Adrielle to *death.*" Larel sneered, her calculated triumph sending a white-hot poker of rage into my heart.

The executioner assumed the position, waiting for the command. The axe gleamed in the sunlight, sharp and deadly.

If I was going to do something, now would be the time.

"The Lor'andann was possessed by a tantankai!" I cried.

The crowd fell silent and began to mutter to one another.

"Lies!" Larel shouted. "Where is your proof, *shride*? You have none!"

"You want proof?" I shouted. "I'll give you proof!"

I struggled against the guards holding my arms as my power coiled within.

Set me free. Set me free. Set me free.

Okay, I thought. *But remember… Larel is our enemy. No other.*

The veil wrapped around me and the collar shattered, the pieces falling onto the platform. The guards let me go, staggering backwards in surprise.

Larel's eyes widened as I changed before her, my skin shimmering blue and the black tar of the veil growing over my fingers, over my hand, and up my arms.

I'd never felt death so strong before. It was like ice flowing through my veins, the currents shrieking at me to feed them souls to carry away. There were so many just standing there waiting to be taken.

"*Liash li Ashli!*" Larel staggered backwards. "No! You're with them. You—"

I swept my arm through the air and tore away her illusion, baring her true face to the people of Un Alari. As she fell to her knees, the assembled Fae cried out in shock.

"Chimera," I rasped. "*Chimera!*"

"Lies!" Larel wailed, desperately trying to hold onto her deception. "You've come to end us all!"

"Why lie when the truth is more powerful?" I asked, advancing on her. "You murdered my father, took my mother, and hunted my people. You twisted the soul of the Lor'andann and tormented him with a tantankai. You manipulated the people of Un Alari into believing the spirits were the elementals. You killed so many people and for what? Power? Wealth? A new world full of glory? You failed to mention the part where the old one had to burn and everyone had to die in order for it to be remade." I looked down on her with disdain. "You are nothing, Larel. Your fanatical sect is pathetic. The Chimera will *never* win. And do you want to know why?" I turned to the people of Un Alari, my black eyes drawing them in. "I am the *Liash li Ashli*… and I am here to help you. I am here to protect this world and rid it of the one thing trying to destroy it. *The Chimera.*"

The people of Un Alari were silent. The influence of the tantankai should have dissolved by now, but they seemed to be tied to it still.

"I am the *Liash li Ashli*, and I declare for the side

of good." Calling on the veil, I reached out and grasped Larel around the neck. "Tell them… Tell them your truth, Larel."

"I-I summoned it," the Fae stammered. "I summoned a tantankai to latch onto the broken soul of the Lor'andann."

The crowd began to jostle forwards and the guards formed a line, separating us.

"Why?" I demanded. "You cannot escape the final judgement of death. The people of Un Alari deserve to know what you did to them."

"It fed on his pain!" she cried, struggling against my power. Her skin shimmered with silver flecks, the grey paling. "I summoned the spirit of Ylyndar and anchored him to it to strengthen the wraith's bond. To torment the Lor'andann!"

"*Why?*"

"To take his power. To enslave his people. To take Un Alari for the Chimera." She gasped as I let her go and fell in a heap beside the block, trembling.

Turning to the guards, I pointed to Larel. "You know what to do."

But they didn't move. They looked at one another, their fear of me outweighing any need they had to fulfil their duty. *Talk about an occupational hazard.*

The executioner grunted in annoyance and shoved past them. He grabbed Larel, forcing her to stand.

"You're making a mistake!" she shrieked, but her cries fell on deaf ears.

I grabbed the collar around Altrys's neck and pulled it as hard as I could. He staggered a step, then the metal shattered, freeing him. Then I turned to Adrielle and held out my blackened hand.

She stared up at me with wide eyes, though she didn't hesitate. She reached out with trembling fingers and took my hand in hers. As I helped Adrielle to her feet, the air seemed to shift and all at once, the people of Un Alari became animated.

"The Chimera are not welcome here!" someone cried.

"Death to the Chimera!"

"Take her head!"

I'd underestimated how loved Adrielle was here, despite her being a Shri'danann. It was her acceptance of me that made them believe, not the absence of the tantankai.

Altrys pressed his hand against her shoulder. "Are you all right?"

"Yes." Adrielle nodded. Her gaze shifted to me. "I knew you'd do it."

"Not quite," I said, staring at Larel's ugly grey face through hazy eyes.

Adrielle looked up at Altrys, her cheeks flushing. "You have the authority here, *Shr'lei*. The people will listen."

He nodded and looked to me.

"I revealed myself as you wished," I told him. "The Chimera are exposed. The law dictates what should happen next."

"I knew I was right about you," he murmured. "That day in the forest…"

I tensed, remembering what Adrielle had said to me yesterday. *It's not because of his oath.*

Altrys didn't notice. He turned towards the crowd and held out his hands.

"People of Un Alari!" The people began to settle, their eyes focusing on him. "As *Shr'lei de Delei'an,* I would take Larel to the capital to be judged, however… I pass that judgement on to you. What say you?"

There was a moment of silence that seemed to stretch into infinity. A thousand people stood together in the centre of the village, none of them breathing a word until…

"*Ash!*" a voice cried.

The Fae word for death.

Then the crowd began to chant, "*Ash, ash, ash, ash!*"

The executioner shoved Larel down onto the block and raised his axe. Then, he swung.

I stood in the hall outside of the Lor'andann's bedroom watching as a healer tended to him.

The day had faded and the sconces had been lit, their light casting a warm glow on the silver stag banners hanging on the wall beside me.

I played with a strand of my emerald hair and

sighed as I caught sight of Altrys walking towards me. He wore his cloak, his shiny *tuathade'shri* badge pinned where everyone could see it.

"Has the healer finished?" he asked, standing beside me.

I shook my head. "No."

Altrys frowned and pressed his hand on the hilt of the knife at his waist. My own had been returned and I felt its comforting weight echo his touch.

"What?" I asked. "You've got a look on your face that I don't like."

"We have a problem."

"Another one?" I groaned. "I'm tired of problems."

"This one cannot wait." He glanced at the Lor'andann through the door and sighed. "Justice must be served for Ylyndar."

I pursed my lips together. At least it wasn't news of a Chimera army marching on Un Alari. I might have blown a fuse if he'd told me that. I hadn't slept in three days, barely eaten, and I stunk like I hadn't washed in a month. I was so ready for this to be over.

"He must answer for his crime and a new Lor'andann must be chosen," Altrys told me.

"I know," I murmured. "It's just… He was the guy we were trying to save."

"No, he wasn't. We were here to save Un Alari."

He was right about everything. Altrys had a blunt way of doing things, but it all worked out in the end.

"Don't tell me you have to stick around," I said. "I

don't like the idea of hitch-hiking all the way to the capital on my own."

He smiled and looked into the Lor'andann's bedroom. "No. An interim Lor'andann will be chosen and the people will make a judgement as the law dictates. Once the queen is notified of what happened here, she will decide who becomes the new Lor'andann."

"I didn't even know his real name," I murmured.

"Ruvyn. His name was Ruvyn."

"It's a shame it had to end this way."

"Was it?"

I nodded. "It seems so unfulfilling. Who won here, Altrys?"

"Un Alari," he replied. "We freed them from the Chimera, despite the harm it could have done to us. That is the sacrifice our place in this world demands of us, and we do it willingly, knowing it is for the greater good."

"Is that what they teach you at *Shr'lei de Delei'an* school?"

Altrys smirked. "It is a little self-righteous, but it works."

The healer shuffled to the door and glanced at Altrys before his gaze landed on me. I couldn't help but see the apprehension in his eyes.

"*Shr'lei*," he said, bowing his head.

"Will he recover?" Altrys asked.

"Yes. He will regain his mind. The Lor'andann

will be fit for judgement in a few days. Until then, he is bound and cannot move from his bed."

Altrys nodded. "Thank you. You may go."

I leaned back against the wall, lowering my gaze as the healer scurried away.

They were afraid of me. I couldn't help but wonder if I'd done the right thing. I'd given away my one chance at anonymity and soon, everyone would know. Wherever I went, I would be a thing to fear.

Altrys moved beside me and raised my chin with a finger. "People will see what you did here, Elspeth," he said, his silver eyes meeting mine. "They will see past your emerald hair and your command of death. They will see your heart. You are more than death… so much more."

A cough at the end of the hall forced us apart.

"Excuse the interruption, *Shr'lei*," a woman called out, "but dinner is served in the hall."

Altrys waved her away, never taking his eyes from me.

"Are you hungry?" he asked.

"No." My stomach rumbled, betraying me.

"Come." He slid his arm around my waist, the touch a little too familiar after what I'd done. "Tonight is for celebrating. Let us worry about the rest in the morning."

17

———

Despite feeling exhausted, I couldn't sleep.

I'd been given a room in the Lor'andann's house, as had Altrys, but the uneasiness I felt after the execution hadn't left me.

The Un Alari guard had swept the village and surrounding forests for any sign of the Chimera, and had found nothing. If anyone else apart from the four men Altrys and I fought had been working with Larel, they were long gone.

I wasn't in a hurry to find them. They would come looking for me sooner or later, but I hoped I'd be in the capital by then. Now that I had some downtime, I was fretting for Rory and Ignis... longing for the simplicity of the Warren.

Walking through the early morning streets of Un Alari, I kept my head down, but it did no good. After all the excitement of the previous day, I was stared at openly, and Fae crossed the street as I approached.

It was difficult not to take it personally, but they didn't understand. It was like the point Altrys had made about Larel and the Chimera. They would believe the story fed to them about the *Liash li Ashli* until I had the chance to make them see otherwise. Until then, I was the Grim Reaper of Un Alari, stalking the streets for an unsuspecting soul to eat.

Around me, work went on as normal. Merchants opened shops, the tavern threw open its doors, stable hands worked tirelessly, farmers brought their produce into town, and the washerwomen waded into the river.

White sheets hung on lines and in the trees, the fabric flapping in the gentle breeze as the sun dried the water from the fibres. It was a calm scene, the river flowing as fast as it always had, the forest stretching into the distance, and the mountains towering over it all.

I lingered amongst the field of sheets, my hair fluttering around muddy shoulders. For a moment, I thought about using an illusion or putting up my hood, but it was no use. Everyone knew what I was now.

Saria stood in the water, rinsing soap suds from a long strip of fabric. Her skirts were hitched up to stop them from getting wet, but the hem was still damp, the current tugging at them every time she bent over. A few other women worked on the shore, some I recognised from the other day, but they didn't notice me.

I took a deep breath. If I could stand up before the whole village and stop an execution, then certainly I could talk to one woman.

"Saria?"

The De'ashlide looked up from her work and frowned when she saw me standing by the shore. There was a familiar flash of fear in her eyes and I glanced away.

"I'm sorry I had to deceive you," I said. "It was to help Un Alari."

She said nothing.

"If I had told you the truth, you would still look at me like I am evil incarnate… just as you are now." I forced myself to look at her. "I didn't ask to be born this way. Nor did I ask for some stupid prophecy to hang over my head. I'm sick and tired of trying to defend myself, Saria. I've sacrificed everything to save others, yet they still fear me." I sighed and shook my head. "Sometimes I wonder why I keep fighting. I'm so tired…"

Water splashed and Saria stood before me. "How long has it been since you've slept?"

I looked at her, wondering where this was going.

"*Ailain li*," she said.

I frowned, not understanding.

Saria sighed and offered me a small smile. "*Ailain li* is a root that will help you sleep," she explained. "Ask someone in the kitchen at the Lor'andann's house, they should have some they can brew into a tea for you. They will add some *mille* petals, too."

My throat tightened, but I managed a croaky thank you.

"You're not from this world, are you?" she asked. "You lived in the other place?"

I wasn't sure how much to say, but I nodded. It was her story about the Lor'andann that helped me and Altrys free the village, so I owed her that much at least.

"*Ailain li,*" she told me. "Don't forget."

Maybe she forgave me. Maybe she understood me. Maybe she just simply tried to do all those things in her own way. Or maybe she didn't want to at all.

I guess I would never know.

The village had become more animated by the time I managed to gather the courage to cross the bridge.

I spotted Adrielle outside of the tavern, leaning against the balustrade of the veranda. Her pink hair was pinned up in tight ringlets and her silver corset clung firmly to her lithe waist, giving the illusion that she had curves.

I found myself thinking of Altrys's story and I almost turned around and walked the other way, but she saw me.

"Elspeth!" she called, waving me over. "I did not expect to see you."

"I had nowhere else to be," I replied with a shrug.

"It isn't my place to listen in on the affairs of your people."

"Neither is it mine," she said with a smile. "Would you like to come in? We have food and a beautiful new *aru'de* from the east. I've already seen you taste it and you *love it*."

My eyes widened. "Have not."

Adrielle laughed. "You caught me there."

I looked through the tavern doors, desperately wanting to go in. "I have no money."

She waved a hand at me. "*Shride* eat and drink for free."

"But I'm not…" I sighed. "You're not afraid of me?"

"Of course not. I'm not one to believe stories over the things I've seen with my own eyes." She wrapped an arm around my shoulders and guided me up onto the verandah and into the tavern.

It was far too early for there to be many patrons, but Adrielle still sat me by the bar and set down a mug of *aru'de* in front of me.

"How are you?" I asked. "After yesterday?"

"I'm perfectly all right. It was frightening to be sure, but I had faith in you."

"Is it that easy to deal?" I wondered. "I will never forget the moment the axe came down on Larel's neck, knowing it could have been yours instead."

"Altrys, you mean," she corrected.

"I won't lie. I don't know how to feel about you, Adrielle, but I don't want anyone to die. I've only ever taken a life to protect myself or others. Larel may have deserved what she got, but I never relished it." Nor did the moment her soul was thrust across the veil feel satisfying, far from it.

Adrielle's eyes flashed silver. "Since this is the last time we will have to talk, I wanted to thank you, Elspeth."

I sipped at the wine, anything to hide the fact that I was uncomfortable. Tangy flavours of tropical fruits played across my taste buds, the *aru'de* reminding me of a syrupy piña colada.

"I know Altrys told you about what happened between us," Adrielle went on, revealing she had another vision—or she was reading my body language with the skill inherent in all bartenders. "I hope you don't hold it against me. It was a long time ago, and if I could have done things differently…"

"So, do you still love him?" I set down the mug, still oblivious to what she was thanking me for exactly.

"I love the memory of him, I see that now." Her gaze met mine. "He has changed, grown for the better. I am no longer his equal and it does no good to dwell in the past. Altrys… he is my better." She leaned against the bar and studied me so intently, I shied away. "You have a fractured destiny, Elspeth. I feel as if anything could happen."

"I have a prophecy," I told her. "There is no fractured destiny for me."

She smiled dreamily and twirled her finger around a pink curl. "Prophecies are just words. Words can be interpreted a multitude of different ways. Watch for the cracks, Elspeth. They are not what they seem."

It was the second time she'd said something like that and the uneasiness in the pit of my stomach grew.

She is not who she seems. They are not what they seem.

In other words, I couldn't trust anyone—Rory and Ignis had it without a doubt, but what about Altrys?

Adrielle nodded. "You can trust him, too."

"Are you sure?"

"Oh, yes." She grinned and pressed her palms against her flushed cheeks.

I gave her an incredulous look and set down the *aru'de*. I was so drunk.

"Ah, here comes Altrys," she said, causing my heart to misfire.

The stool beside me scraped back and Altrys sat, taking the mug away from me. "I warned you about Adrielle and her *aru'de*." To prove he was joking, he finished off the rest of the wine and grinned at me.

"You are such a man," Adrielle complained, fetching another mug for me. "Elspeth doesn't need anyone to tell her what to do."

I didn't like the easy banter between them, and I scowled. "What happens now? I can't stay here now that the Chimera know I've declared myself."

"Well, firstly, the interim Lor'andann has been chosen," Altrys told us.

"Oh? Was it Theodas?" Adrielle asked.

Altrys nodded. To me he said, "Theodas is a cousin of Ruvyn."

"Is that wise?" I asked. "Asking family to take over?"

"Ylyndar was a good man, Elspeth," he replied. "Theodas is as well. It was voted unanimously by the merchants and families of Un Alari. They know their people best."

"I'm glad," Adrielle said. "He will do well. Niarisshia would do us honour if she chose him to retain the title."

He nodded his agreement. "And secondly, Elspeth is right. She needs to leave Un Alari as soon as possible."

I downed a large mouthful of wine.

"We have been granted provisions, mounts, and a detachment of guards to escort us back to the capital," he added, watching me with a raised eyebrow. "We'll be leaving at dawn… unless you have any pressing matters keeping you here."

My heart skipped several beats. "You're coming with me?"

"Of course."

I said nothing, not wanting to betray the multitude of feelings vying for my attention.

Altrys frowned, then glanced away. "Adrielle, I was hoping to speak with you before I left."

I almost choked on my wine and pushed the mug away. "I'm going back to bed," I said hastily. "I didn't get any sleep last night. Uh… I suppose this is goodbye, Adrielle."

"*A'ladrei*, Elspeth," the Shri'danann said. "I hope you fare well on your journey."

I looked up at her and nodded. "And you, Adrielle."

Leaving them in peace, I scurried across the tavern and lingered in the doorway. Outside, the air felt free now the tantankai was gone, though I wished it was absent of a thousand other things.

Looking over my shoulder, I watched Altrys and Adrielle for a moment. She was smiling and leaning over the bar, her fingers tracing over his jaw. He laughed, the sound forcing my gaze away.

I gave myself a moment to feel it… then I left them to say their goodbyes.

18

We departed Un Alari the following morning as the first rays of the sun coloured the horizon.

Our band was made up of me, Altrys, and six male guards. They didn't wear full armour, but a mixture of steel plate and leather, their chests emblazoned with the silver stag of Un Alari. Their bows and swords meant business, adding a layer of deterrent for any unsavoury characters we might meet on the road. Though having a *Shr'lei de Delei'an* amongst our number was message enough.

I'd been given a handsome horse with a dappled grey and white coat. Its hair was dense and springy like moss, and its mane was long and silver. I'd never ridden before and had struggled to find my seat in the saddle, but the animal seemed content to follow whatever tail was in front of it.

We took the main road out of the town, through

the forest, and headed towards the lower bound of mountains to the south.

Altrys rode next to me, in the centre of the band, and cast sidelong glances at me.

Finally tired of his fleeting looks, I asked him which way we would be going.

"Right now, we are in the Northern Reaches," he explained. "We must travel through the mountain pass, down into the valleys of Lith'lander, across the plains of Delliare, then follow the coast to the capital."

"Two thousand leagues," I said with a groan. "How long is that going to take?"

"Your arse isn't used to a saddle?"

I choked on my own spit and coughed.

Altrys grinned. "See? I do learn things from you, Elspeth Odhweine."

I'd created a monster.

"How long will it take?" I asked again.

"Three weeks, if nothing befalls us."

Well, it seemed a league wasn't as far as a nautical league on Earth. Even then I didn't know how long that was, just that it was longer than a mile, though I was used to kilometres having grown up in Australia.

Still, three weeks was a long time and a lot could happen. I hoped this was one of those moments where we'd get a montage, but real life wasn't a movie with a cut scene. The Chimera knew I was here, and like a bad smell, they'd be back.

I shifted in my saddle, making the leather creak. Altrys was right, my arse already hurt.

"I wish I could phase us there," I complained. "But I have no idea what the capital looks like."

"It wouldn't work?"

"No, I don't think so. I've always gone to places I've seen before. If I tried… who knows where we might end up."

"Safer to risk the blisters, then."

I grimaced and pulled up the hood of my cloak.

From then on, I kept my hair hidden, thinking it wiser not to use my Colour to hide it. The days were long, and my muscles ached twenty-four-seven.

Three weeks was beginning to feel like three years.

On the surface, the Fae world was just like the one I'd come from, but there were so many subtle differences it was hard to keep count of them all. The flowers were large and colourful, the birds were larger and almost like shiny metallic objects soaring through the sky, the buildings and farms were reminiscent of Medieval architecture, and the Fae we encountered on the road were more colourful and diverse than any I'd met in Un Alari.

It wasn't exactly backpacking across Europe, but the things I'd seen so far beat out anything Paris and Prague could ever have to offer.

When we camped at night, the lush forests of

Lith'lander were alive with sprites and Fae creatures that were neither Shri'danann nor De'ashlide. Altrys told me stories of the Dreamweavers of Delliare, feline-esque people who lived on the open plains… where Yenris'del must have lived before she met my father.

All of us were a long way from home.

The Fae world was opening up and with it, came more dangers than just the Chimera. Depending on where we travelled, the Unseelie were seen as untrustworthy amongst the Seelie and the De'ashlide. My hair marked me, so I remained hidden amongst our group, staying silent and small—something I'd honed all those years ago as a bullied kid in high school.

The guards treated me with a distant respect, only talking to me enough to make sure they weren't lax in their duties in front of Altrys. Any attempts I made to put them at ease or be friendly or even to learn their names were met with polite brush-offs. After a few days of trying, I gave up.

I busied myself with learning how to do small things, like make a campfire, gut a fish, unsaddle my horse, how to brush out its coat and check its hooves for rocks. It was a world away from the modern life I'd had in Sydney where food came from supermarkets and cars dominated the roads.

A week after we'd left Un Alari, we made camp in a clearing a short distance from the main road.

I made a little fire away from the guard, busying

myself with my bedroll. Sleeping on the ground in a magical forest wasn't exactly as romantic as it sounded. It still got cold, it was still dirty, and ants and bugs existed in this world, too.

My hair fell into my eyes and I brushed it back angrily.

Altrys appeared on the other side of my little fire and dumped his bag and blankets beside mine.

"You've been quiet for the last few days," he said.

"I'm not used to travelling like this." I shrugged and scraped my hair back again. "I guess I'm just tired."

He looked at me for a moment. "Sit down."

I didn't have it in me to argue. I crumpled onto my bedroll and crossed my aching legs.

Altrys sat behind me, stretching his legs out on either side of me and combed his fingers through my hair. Back on Earth, most men would see this act of styling a woman's hair as a moment of weakness, but Altrys didn't think twice. Neither did the guards. They barely looked at us as he tugged my emerald locks into a tight braid.

He didn't say anything as he worked, and when he was done, he fastened the end with a leather tie like the one that had matted into his little dreadlocked braids long ago.

I ran my hand over my hair. "You did a good job. I'm surprised."

"So?"

"It's strange for a man to braid hair."

"If you hadn't noticed, most men keep their hair long," he murmured, leaning close. "Is it not the same where you come from?"

I shook my head. "Most men keep their hair short."

Altrys seemed to find this amusing. "Long hair is not seen to be masculine? How strange."

Men and women seemed to be equals here on many fronts, though their divisions came more from magic than gender. Same problems, different name, I guessed.

"What is it like in your world?" Altrys asked, standing and repositioning himself beside me.

I thought for a moment. "Well, there's magic there, but it isn't open like it is here. Most people are human… uh, like De'ashlide."

"Not open?"

"Humans don't know about magic," I explained. "There are billions of people living all over the world, but only a few are magical. My world is one of science and machines. There's noise, pollution, and huge cities. There are almost two hundred different countries."

Altrys curled his nose. "That sounds awful."

"There's beauty, too."

"Beauty in secrecy?" He shook his head. "There is no freedom in hiding who you are."

The light had faded around us as we talked and night had arrived. Stars twinkled through the tree canopy above, hanging like jewels in a cloudless sky.

Two guards lingered in the shadows, a sentry for the wilds north of our camp and one for the road at the south. The remaining four huddled around their fire, cooking and drinking. They laughed at intervals, their chatter too low to hear. Even if I could, I still didn't understand much of the Fae language.

"Would you return?" Altrys asked, his arm pressing against mine.

"I have family there."

"Ah, your Druid family." He sounded disappointed.

"There is a lot to do here," I told him. "Thinking about that is more than enough for now. Who knows how long the fight against the Chimera will take?"

"Elspeth."

I looked up at him and he edged towards me. His fingers brushed against my cheek and I before I could take a breath, he kissed me.

All I could think was, *Why me?* I was plain. I wasn't beautiful. I was Unseelie. I was death. I was the herald of the end of the world, and Altrys was strong, handsome, intelligent, and kind. *Why me?*

He drew back slightly, his lips brushing mine with a message that told me he didn't want to stop any time soon, but my cheeks flushed and I looked away. My heart hammered in an unbearable rhythm, wanting to draw him to me, yet push him away.

"Don't be shy, Elspeth," Altrys murmured. "You are so courageous in battle, but this frightens you?"

"Of course, it frightens me, Altrys. It's not that I have little experience, it's…" My throat tightened.

"*Liash li Ashli,*" he whispered.

"I don't know what kind of future we could have," I murmured. "I have so much going against me. If there's an after… I just don't know."

"Thinking of the future keeps one from living in the now," he whispered. "Now is all anyone has, Elspeth."

I couldn't speak. I couldn't think.

Altrys pressed his fingers underneath my chin, coaxing me to look up. "Do you remember what you said to me the day after you saved my life?"

I shook my head, catching his silver gaze.

"You said, *you know* what *I am. You know nothing of* who *I am or* why *I am.*"

"Altrys—"

"You have these moments of fierceness," he went on, "as if nothing can stop you, but then there are times you shrink in on yourself. It's as if you believe you do not deserve any happiness because of what you are."

I tensed. Rory had said the same thing to me back when we'd first met, though not quite as eloquently.

"I don't want to hurt anyone," I said. "But I'm destined to do just that. I'm reminded of it every time I look in the mirror and every time I look into another person's eyes. I see their fear and they're right to be scared."

Altrys took my hand in his. "It doesn't matter

what others think about you. They have their own fears to deal with. You cannot force them to understand, just as much as you cannot force someone to love. Some people will always choose to believe a lie even if they see the truth, simply because it is easier."

"Or they fear that the lie is true," I whispered.

"You can only be true to yourself, Elspeth. Let go of your doubts and do as your heart and mind dictate. Let your intuition guide you. It did not lead you astray in Un Alari." He pressed his forehead against mine. "I have faith that you will choose the right path. A prophecy is merely words. It only means something if someone believes in it."

Did I believe in the prophecy simply because I feared my uncertain future? That it was easier to believe the prophecy than face the feelings I had when I looked at Altrys?

We'd met ten days ago. *Ten days.*

"Altrys… I'm afraid."

He cupped my cheek. "So am I."

I took a deep breath in an attempt to find some courage and my whole body went rigid as I felt a soul slip away. It passed through the veil with a sigh—a soft, secret death.

Tearing away from Altrys, I grabbed my knife, my power rising. They were out there, in the dark.

"Elspeth?" He rose to one knee, his hand reaching for his sword.

"Chimera," I rasped. "*They found us.*"

19

———

I slammed my palm down onto the ground, pushing my Colour into the earth.

There was no time to care about what I was revealing, only that everyone would die if I didn't.

An electric blue prism coiled into life, bursting from the ground around the camp, the geometric lines crackling with the potent magic of the Fae. The Colour spread upwards, uncovering the Chimera hiding in the darkness.

The Un Alari guard scrambled to their feet, drawing their swords.

"Chimera! *Ah'ila! Ah'ila!*" they cried.

The enemy rushed out of the shadows, attacking at full force.

The sound of steel clashing against steel filled the clearing and magic ebbed all around. The web had given us light, but had also trapped the Chimera here with us, and now we'd fight until one was defeated.

Altrys turned, delivering a quick strike to a Chimera's arm and I ducked a blow that came towards my front. My knife slashed at the male Fae's thigh, drawing blood, and as he buckled, I slammed the blade into his sickly grey neck.

They hadn't even bothered to hide behind their illusions, using their grotesque faces as a weapon. The guard fought wildly, but their movements were sluggish. I couldn't blame them, but looks were nothing compared to a sword flying towards you.

Altrys fought like a Fae possessed, cutting down a Chimera in a tornado of steel. He pulled a small knife from his belt and hurled it across the clearing, a garbled cry signalling it had found its mark.

A Chimera was bearing down on a guard in front of me, and I ran towards them, calling on my Colour. Crystal light splintered along the blade of my knife and I lunged. It slammed upwards into the Fae's back, finding his heart, and the prism crawled into his body and strangled the life out of him. It was a quicker death than the Chimera deserved.

I kicked the body away as I felt the soul depart and held my hand out to the fallen guard. "Are you all right?"

He looked up at me and nodded sharply. Taking my hand, I hauled him to his feet, and we both joined the fight once more.

Altrys thrust his blade through the stomach of a Chimera, pushing him back onto the forest floor with a grunt. The sword made a squelching sound as it pulled free, the length covered in sticky bluish blood.

My senses tingled as the sounds of fighting abated, and I looked down at my hand. The crystals were gone, but I still felt the echo of them tearing through my skin.

"Is that all of them?" one of the guards asked, gasping for breath.

I allowed the prism to fade and it fell back into the earth like silk, the Colour feeding back into me. Simple firelight warmed the bloody scene.

One Fae was dead, a few carried minor wounds, but the Chimera had suffered a mass defeat.

The guards were looking at me with a newfound respect, but I wasn't paying attention to them. My senses vibrated as the forest whispered, telling me of dark things approaching.

I stared out into the darkness and murmured, "More are coming."

"How many?" Altrys asked.

"I don't know." I shrugged. "At least as many, if not more."

"There's a garrison not far from here on the coast," the guard captain said. "We'll get there in twenty minutes if we ride hard."

I didn't have to ask why we weren't staying there for the night. They wanted my movements to be secret, but the Chimera had found us anyway, despite not using my abilities until now.

"What about your man?" I asked.

"There's nothing we can do for him now," the guard told me. "We'll come back for him."

"If we get out of this," another guard said.

"Altrys and I will take the rear," I said. "If they gain, I can slow them down."

"Agreed." The captain nodded and turned to the remaining men. "Let's saddle up!"

We barely had enough time to gather our things and saddle the horses before we heard the Chimera's approach.

Mounting up, we galloped down the road, the jolting of my horse almost knocking me off my saddle. I wasn't used to riding, let alone fleeing for my life in the ultimate steeple chase.

I tightened my grip on the reins, squeezed my thighs around the horse's middle, and held on for dear life.

The road twisted and turned through the forest, low hanging branches clawing at us as we passed. Here and there, the thick growth parted to reveal stunning views of the moonlit coast—a white beach bordered by ragged cliffs and a tower pointing towards the sky.

The road opened up and the guards galloped ahead. I sensed the Chimera were gaining and I had to do something to slow them down or—

Altrys slumped forwards and his horse veered to the side. An arrow protruded from his back, almost buried to the fletching.

I gasped and looked over my shoulder at the Chimera, who were a lot closer than I'd expected. A man was standing high on his saddle, a bow in his hands, and a battalion of grey-skinned monsters behind him.

"Altrys, hold on!" I shouted.

I kicked my horse, tugging the reins to the right, and reached for the bridle of Altrys's mount. The moment my fingers brushed against the leather, another arrow flew out of the darkness and slammed into his shoulder.

Altrys cried out in shock, his gaze meeting mine… and then he fell.

What came next seemed to happen in slow motion. Altrys collided with the ground and rolled, the arrows grinding into his body as he tumbled. His horse neighed and sprinted off wildly, my own spooking and joining the wild gallop.

Behind us, the Chimera slowed, their horses circling the fallen Shr'lei.

I jerked hard on my reins and the grey horse skidded. I leapt off its back before I was thrown forwards, landing lithely on the road. The horse threw its head into the air, its eyes rolling, and I drew my knife, my anger driving my feet to the one place Altrys would want me to run from.

"Let him go!" I shouted, striding towards the Chimera—all twenty of them.

They dismounted and their horses moved away into the forest. They began to laugh amongst themselves as they saw the knife in my hand. *What could this little girl do with that tiny thing?*

The Chimera, who seemed to be their leader, shoved Altrys to the ground, grinding his boot into his back.

"You for the *Shr'lei*," he said. "That is our bargain, *Liash li Ashli.*"

"Elspeth, *no*," Altrys cried, causing the Chimera to strike him hard enough to render him unconscious.

"You don't get it, do you?" I murmured, my hands shaking with coiled rage. "Mindel never understood what he was dealing with, and that's why he lost."

"Mindel did not lose, Elspeth." The Chimera's grin widened. "He brought you to us."

These people were egomaniacs. They had a manipulation to try to convince me everything I did was tied to some mystical prophecy—that I had no free will.

"Then you must learn the same lesson he did." I raised my hands and called on the veil. "You cannot bargain with the *Liash li Ashli.*"

"Death is not the end, Elspeth," he told me. "You will be ushering in a new world where all souls will be reborn into glory."

"*Let him go.*"

"There is no place for the *shr'lei*. Unbelievers will not find their way. He will die a true death." He grabbed the end of one of the arrows and twisted it. Altrys groaned, his fingers clawing at the road as he tried to stay awake.

I could smell his blood in the air and felt the veil reach for his soul.

My skin began to chill, and the veil's thick tar dripped from my fingertips. I could do it. I could unleash the veil and save Altrys. I could control it here. If I didn't, they would kill him—if his injuries didn't claim him first.

The ghost of his kiss still lingered on my lips. *You are so courageous in battle, but this frightens you?*

"I will kiss you again, Altrys, *Shr'lei de Delei'an*," I whispered. "And I will never be afraid of loving again." I took a step forwards and raised my hand. "I am the veil between life and death. Life and the Chimera."

The enemy tensed, their fear unmistakable. Did they really think I wouldn't fight? Did they think I was weak? *Did they think I was like them?*

Kill them, choke them, drown them, the black sun whispered.

"I warned you, Chimera," I rasped, my vision misting. "I warned you this would happen."

A few Fae at the rear of the group fell to their knees and prayed.

"Get up!" the leader shrieked. "She will come! Do not falter! Faith, Chimera!" He reached for the arrows in Altrys's back, but I was faster.

I closed my fist and they all fell to their knees, gasping for breath. "I don't want to kill, but I will if it means protecting this world." The Chimera clawed at their necks as my power strangled them. "I will kill all of you if it means protecting *him*."

The veil oozed around their waists and I stood in front of their leader, my rage barely holding the black sun in check.

"I imprisoned Mindel and the Chimera on Earth in death, but you…" I sneered down at him, my vision hazy. "You I will end right here."

Black tar seeped upwards, coiling around the legs of the fallen Chimera. It circled around Altrys, honouring my pleas, and consumed the enemy one by one.

Cracks appeared across their skin as the life was dragged from their bodies. Their souls dissolved through the veil, screaming and tearing for me as they went, but I was cold to it, their deaths passing with nothing more than a trickle of ice down my spine.

Finally, nothing was left of their earthly bodies but dried husks, shells that housed fanatical monsters who cared nothing for the lives they took.

That was the difference between us. I cared, I didn't relish what I had to do in order to survive. The Chimera basked in the blood of their enemies.

The wind stirred, carrying the cleansing aura of nature along with it. The forest ebbed with cool, green light, and I gasped as I saw movement amongst the trees. The elementals had called the wind to carry the ash of the Chimera away.

The sound of thundering hooves echoed up the road, growing louder as they approached.

Altrys, Shr'lei de Delei'an, they whispered. *Ak'ande la.*

I collapsed next to Altrys, my skin fading from blue to flushed pink as the veil retreated.

"Don't die," I whispered, smoothing his hair back. "Please, Altrys, don't die."

There was so much blood. I pressed my hands around the arrow wounds and called on my Colour. Rory had only taught me basic healing, and this went beyond that.

Warmth spread through my palms as I focused on my intent. *Stop the bleeding.*

I was barely aware of the world around me as a dozen horses circled us.

Stop the bleeding.

Someone barked orders as I pressed down on Altrys's wounds.

Stop the bleeding.

A man knelt beside us, the clink of his armour startling me.

"*E'dreha,* Elspeth Odhweine," he said.

I stared up at the man, my eyes wide. He had a badge like Altrys's emblazoned on his breastplate—an eight-pointed silver star—and short-cropped hair the colour of crimson.

"I'm Elion, *Shr'lei de Delei'an,*" he told me. "Queen Niarisshia sends her regards."

The queen? "Altrys… He's alive, but…"

"He will be given the best care." Elion gestured to the soldiers. "Where are the Chimera?"

I glanced down at the ash and swallowed hard. "You're kneeling on them."

20

———————

The tower on the cliff was named Ad Valrah—the Iron Pinnacle.

Even though it faced the ocean, it was warm inside, until random gusts of salty wind blasted through the gaps in the window. The fire buffeted in the hearth, sending sparks up the chimney.

I sat beside a cot in the small room, the smell of herbs and healing balms heavy in the air.

Altrys lay in the bed, his shoulder tightly bound. Blood had seeped through the bandages where the arrows had broken through his chest, but that was to be expected. He'd bled a lot and the prisms I'd used were almost depleted.

The healer was a gnarled, bent over man with the remnants of vibrant orange hair amongst the grey. He was a skilled Shri'danann, enlisted by the *Shr'lei de Delei'an* to tend to Altrys's wounds.

He'd fussed over the *shr'lei* as he'd taken out the

arrows, his gaze flickering to mine several times before he'd pressed a tangy-scented poultice over each entry and exit wound, then had two of the soldiers assist with wrapping bandages around Altrys's shoulder.

I had lingered in the corner, sensing the magic as the Fae worked, but said nothing. Altrys hardly made a sound, floating in and out of consciousness as they worked. Now, he was asleep.

The healer had nodded at me once—a short, sharp motion shrouded in a mixture of acknowledgement and apprehension. He knew I'd used unknown magic to stop the bleeding, and he knew I was the *Liash li Ashli*.

That was also how I knew Altrys would be okay. His soul was firmly lodged in his body and wouldn't be going anywhere anytime soon.

I studied his features, surprised at how young he looked when he was asleep. He had more than just the one scar on his jaw, too. There was a small knick in his left eyebrow and several slashes across his lean torso—one on his side, another on his abdomen, and a jagged line on his right shoulder.

He'd lived a hard life fighting in the queen's name.

"The elementals came," I told him. "The real elementals this time. You should have seen them, Altrys. Well, not that I saw much. There was a light from within the forest and their shadows came. They called the wind to sweep away the ash of the Chimera." I bit my bottom lip. "They said your name."

I didn't know much about the elementals, except for the fact that they were revered as the next closest thing to gods. One thing I did understand about the Fae is that they worshipped things that were tangible… and real. The proof being that the Chimera were nuts about me.

Altrys eyes fluttered open and he stirred, grimacing at the tightness in his shoulder.

"Don't move," I told him. "You need to let yourself heal."

"Elspeth," he murmured and his fingers reached for mine. He winced slightly and I grabbed his hand. "What…"

"They're dead." I brushed my fingers over the back of his hand, studying all the curves and creases in his skin. "I killed them."

The fire cracked and a log popped, sending sparks into the chimney.

Altrys tightened his grip on my hand. "I'm sorry you had to, but thankful I'm alive to say it."

A rush of emotions swirled inside me. I let them rise, picking out each one like wildflowers in a field— fear, doubt, lust, need, relief, anger, anxiety, happiness.

"I'm not afraid anymore," I whispered. "I…" I leaned down and pressed my lips against his. "I don't know what this is, but I like being around you. I like talking to you. I just…"

"Elspeth." He tried to sit up, but I pushed him back down. "I'm fine. It was just a couple of arrows."

"*Just* a couple? You fell off your horse."

"I'm going to be okay… and so are you."

"This isn't about me," I told him. "It's about you almost getting killed."

"I didn't al—" He stopped in mid-sentence, his cheeks paling. "You felt my…"

I nodded.

An awkward silence opened between us as the gravity of the path I would have to take settled over us. I'd come so far, yet this was only the beginning. There would be more battles, and bloodier ones than we'd fought in Un Alari and last night.

If Altrys cared about me, he would either let me go or risk everything to come with me. I couldn't ask him to do either. Maybe it was selfish, but I wished we could run away and leave this Chimeric mess behind us for someone else to deal with. But it wasn't in me to leave a whole world to burn when I was the only one who might be able to stop it. I just couldn't.

"What does *ak'ande la*, mean?"

"It means…" His brow furrowed. "Save him."

I smiled. I understood now. The elementals had big plans for Altrys, and I wondered if I should tell him.

"Who said that?" he asked.

"No one." I lowered my gaze, thinking better of it. "I just heard someone say it and it stuck in my head, is all."

I didn't know what else to say, so I went to take my hand from his, but he tightened his grip.

"Elspeth… Would you do just one thing for me?"

"Just one?" I joked.

He nodded. "It's important."

I raised my eyebrows. "Well? What is it?"

"When you go… don't leave me behind."

We departed Ad Valrah the moment Altrys was well enough to travel.

Elion and a detachment of the soldiers garrisoned at the tower came with us, saddled up on elegant horses that stood tall and proud—warhorses.

The Un Alari guard parted ways with us, returning for their fallen comrade before making the journey back to the Silver Mountains.

The *Shr'lei de Delei'an* set a steady pace that tested Altrys's stamina, but he never complained, even though I knew his shoulder troubled him. His training and honour dictated that he never showed weakness where others could see, especially the enemy.

By now my arse cheeks had toughened up some, and I began to enjoy the long days riding.

When we were within a day of the capital, Elion chose to ride beside Altrys and I, leaving his second-in-command to lead the column.

I had gotten to know him little over the past two weeks, and I suspected he was keeping his distance after finding me on the road five miles outside of Ad Valrah, kneeling in Chimera ash.

"The queen will want to speak with you when we

arrive," he told me. "Word has already reached her about the goings-on in Un Alari, but she will want to hear it from you. And you also, Altrys."

"What is she like?" I asked.

"Niarisshia is hard, but fair," he replied. "They are good traits for a queen. She will judge on your person and deeds, not rumour. You have nothing to fear."

"It's not fear exactly," I said. "It's knowing what my blood holds, and what she might ask me to do with it, that I worry about."

"It seems you both have the same agenda," he mused. "The eradication of the Chimera. Or am I mistaken?"

Elion was a stoic man, and he was even more serious in his duties than Altrys. It was impossible to know a Fae's true age, though it seemed to me as if he was at least in his forties or the Fae equivalent. His tone and choice of words leaned towards wisdom that came from age, not books.

Whatever I said next, I had to be careful. This was going into a report for the queen, after all.

"The Chimera have caused a lot of suffering," I said. "They have taken a lot from me, Elion. If they wanted me to join their cause, then they shouldn't have murdered my father." I smiled up at him and fluttered my eyelashes. "How's that?"

Elion frowned. "After what happened in Un Alari, we are on the edge of war."

I rolled my eyes. "Story of my life."

"The capital is on the horizon," Altrys said, breaking apart our tense conversation.

Elion nodded, also thankful for the change in topic. "It is called Sil Astrad. The City of Stars."

"Why is it called that?" The City of Stars sounded romantic, as if the streets were paved with diamonds and liquid gold spurted out of jewel-encrusted fountains.

"You'll see soon enough," Altrys replied with a grin.

Elion moved ahead of us and I raised my eyebrows.

"Do you have a secret report, too?" I asked.

"Every world has its politics, Elspeth," he replied, not surprised I'd picked up on it. "Even I am not immune from it."

I sighed. "Say something nice, okay?"

Altrys laughed. "I don't have to try too hard for that."

"The queen has sent an escort to meet us," Elion said over his shoulder. He pointed towards the city where I spotted a group of mounted Fae cantering towards us. "That's good tidings, Elspeth."

I craned my neck as we neared and soon, I was able to count a dozen riders and see the silver and gold banner flowing above them. It carried the same eight-pointed star that I'd become so familiar with. The *tuathade'shri*—the royal seal.

That's when I felt a familiar pulse of Colour.

"It's Rory," I said, my heart skipping a beat. "Rory's with them."

"The Druid who's in love with you?" Altrys asked a little sullenly.

"You're a *Shr'lei de Delei'an*," I told him. "Don't pout."

"I'm not pouting. It's physically impossible."

"I thought Fae detested lying."

He opened his mouth to retort but was silenced by something in the distance.

"What is that… creature?" he finally managed.

Following his stunned gaze, I spotted a black and blue tiger sprinting down the road towards us, the sun making his crystalline coat sparkle. The soldiers reined in their fancy warhorses as they began to shy at the approach of the big cat, and Elion cursed in Fae.

"Ignis!" I cried, leaping off my horse.

I sprinted towards him, a grin on my face. Altrys called out behind me, but his words were lost on the wind.

Midway between the two groups of riders, I collided with the tiger and we landed in a heap, Ignis's tongue rasping up my cheek as we rolled in the dirt.

Laughing, I wrapped my arms around his neck. "I've missed you so much, you stupid feline."

"Elspeth!"

The sound of Rory's voice echoed across the open road and I rose to my feet just in time. The Druid threw his arms around me and we tightly embraced as

Ignis brushed up against us, his contented purring at a million hundred decibels. It was so good to see them.

Rory's words sprang out in a rush. "I'm so glad you're safe. When you didn't come through the portal, I—"

"It's all right, Rory," I interrupted. "Everything worked out in the end."

"Thank Colour, I heard you had a run in with the Chimera." He drew back, his eyes sparkling.

"Are you *crying?*" I demanded.

"No," he said with a pout. "*Never.*"

The sound of riders bearing down on us pulled us back into reality and our reunion was cut short. I looked up at Altrys before turning back to Rory.

"Well then," I said, "have I got a story to tell you."

"Ditto, Elspeth Odhweine, hero of Un Alari," Rory said. "*Ditto.*"

OTHER BOOKS IN THE DARKLAND DRUIDS

by Nicole R. Taylor

Druids, **Witches**, **Fae**, and **shapeshifters** abound
in this thrilling magical adventure!

Arcane Rising #1
Arcane Spirit #2
Arcane Mythos #3
Arcane Revenant #4

GLOSSARY

Scottish/Irish Gaelic:

please note: the Druids deliberately speak the language in a more formal and pieced together way than fluent Gaelic speakers normally would. This is due to their nomadic heritage spanning across multiple worlds.

- *gealladh* - promise
- *dearbh-aithne* - identity
- *Och, daingead!* - Oh, darn!
- *Tha a ceann anns a 'bhrochan* - Her head is in the porridge (meaning: she's crazy)
- *fàidhean meallta* - false prophets
- *Slàinte* - cheers
- *tha sinn còmhla riut* - we are with you

Fae Terminology & Language:

- *Liash li Ashli* - roughly translates to 'goddess of death'
- *Shri'danann* - the Higher Fae. One of the elite races.
- *De'ashlide* - non-magic Fae.
- *Tuathade'shri* - Royal seal. Represented by

the eight pointed silver star of Queen
Niarisshia.

- *Shr'lei de Delei'an* - Blade of the Queen
- *Lor'andann* - ealdorman/mayor/lord
- *Shride* - deputy
- *Shride de Shr'lei* - Deputy of the Blade
- *A'ladrei* - thank you
- *E'dreha* - greetings (a polite way to say hello
  to a stranger)
- *Aru'de* - wine
- *Bashide* - baby
- *Tantankai* - an ancient parasitic shadow
  wraith that feeds off the pain and suffering
  of its victim.
- *Ashlar an lor* - honour the dead
- *lor'ashlar* - a grave in the form of a stone
  totem holding the ashes of the dead
- *Lor'* - a title of respect similar to a lord
  or lady
- *Un Fall'an* - Silver Stag
- *Ailain li* - a root plant similar to Valerian
- *Mille* - a Fae variety of chamomile
- *Ah'ila* - attack
- *Ak'ande la* - save him

Places:

- Un Alari - the village capital of the Silver Mountains, situated in the Northern Reaches.
- Lith'lander - a lush region of deep valleys and dales bordering the Northern Reaches.
- Delliare - a flat region of grassy plains, home to the feline race of Delliare Dreamweavers.
- Ad Valrah - the Iron Pinnacle.
- Sil Astrad - the City of Stars. The Fae capital.

People (Pronunciation Guide):

- Niarisshia - Ne-ar-iss-hia
- Altrys - Alt-rees
- Larel - Lar-el
- Ylyndar - Ill-en-dar
- Theodas - Theo-das
- Ruvyn - Roo-ven
- Adrielle - Ad-re-elle
- Elion - Ee-leon
- Odhweine - Od-h-ween
- Maerinn - May-rin

Phrases:

- *Leishrilei de tuathade lei li delei'an ash.* - Leave, before I show you the Queen's death.

ABOUT NICOLE

Nicole R. Taylor is an Australian Urban Fantasy author.

She lives in the western suburbs of Melbourne dreaming up nail biting stories featuring sassy witches, duplicitous vampires, hunky shapeshifters, and devious monsters.

She likes chocolate, cat memes, and video games.

When she's not writing, she likes to think of what she's writing next.

Follow Nicole Online:

Website: www.nicolertaylorwrites.com
Facebook: facebook.com/nrtaylorwrites
Newsletter: www.nicolertaylorwrites.com/newsletter
Email: nicole.this.is@gmail.com

ARCANE REVENANT
(THE DARKLAND DRUIDS - BOOK FOUR)

When the black sun rises...nothing is as it seems.

The one place **Elspeth Odhweine** thought she'd find herself, another world wasn't it.

As an honoured guest of the Fae court, she finds herself in the middle of a deadly game of political tug of war. She alone holds the fate of an entire race of magical people in her hands and she will either unite them, or send them to their deaths.

When they receive a lead on their illusive enemy, the Chimera, Elspeth and her friends embark on a treacherous journey to the top of the world in search for answers. She knows she must unravel the truth of her mother's heritage before all she's fought for turns to dust. Trekking across a glacier seems a small thing to do to find the answers she needs to stop the prophecy coming true.

But in the ice and snow lies a truth more deadly than they ever thought possible.

For in the heart of the mountain, death awaits the hand of fate.

Arcane Revenant is the FINAL book of **The Darkland Druids**, *a mystical Urban Fantasy series set in the spellbinding world of the Fae.*

A powerful woman, who is the embodiment of death, travels to another world in order to save it…from herself. Can she stop a devastating war from sweeping across a magical land? Find out in this gripping fantasy saga!

to land in the middle of a prophecy of destruction. Druids, witches, fae, and shapeshifters abound in this thrilling magical adventure!

Find out more at: NicoleRTaylorWrites.com

See what titles are FREE at: Nicole's Free Reads